1.

He was found lying face down, partially stuck in the mud on the sloped bank under the little troll- bridge, in the very shallow river. During the day, you would find hundreds of dog walkers and ramblers enjoying this beautiful part of the Hertfordshire countryside, the children in their droves, paddling and fishing in the water and the wildlife making the most of the lush scenery, with plentiful trees, hedgerow and of course the natural river running through. But this wasn't the middle of the day, this happened in the dead of the night, when the only eyes watching every move are those of the owls, the foxes and the other nocturnal animals, who wait patiently for the day visitors to depart and leave their habitat alone. He was found by the poor guy who spends his days clearing up the crap of the towns' people; the guy who spends the hours when he's not picking up their crap, reminding them on the local facebook group that hanging dog shit in a bag on a tree does not constitute disposing of your dog mess. But he really wasn't expecting to come across a body, especially as the body was virtually naked, only wearing a pair of Tommy Hilfiger boxer shorts.

In fact, Pete, the local street refuse manager (self-titled) had gone for a late night walk after spending 5 hours binge- watching Game of Thrones and smoking himself into oblivion. He had been feeling a little worse for wear after consuming four bags of Doritos and three tubes of Pringles, possibly due to the lack of nutrients in his chosen TV supper and that he'd given himself major cramp in his left leg, having sat on it unknowingly for the best part of the splurge. In his foggy mind, he realised that the only thing he could do next was try and walk off the cramp and open a window or two in his flat to try and get as much fresh air as he could. He had reached the stage where he was fighting through the smoke of his back to back joints to find the window and the key to open it.

And so he took off for a stroll, deep in discussion with himself about who really was in charge of the Seven Kingdoms, and how, even if you were to offer him a million pounds, there is no way in the world he would ever sleep with his own sister. Totally gross, and what the hell would his parents say anyway? He was chuckling to himself as he thought of these preposterous self-inquired questions. Maybe he'd had one drag too much tonight, but he was enjoying his own company and the gentle light from the night sky. If he was lucky, he thought to himself, he might see a badger. Foxes were ten to the penny around here, but despite Badgers being a popular neighbour too, he had only ever seen one, alive that is. He was so engrossed in his thoughts that he almost walked straight past the body en route to his favourite spot where he liked to sit on the bridge, hanging his feet over the water and getting carried away with the calming, almost hypnotic rhythm of the ripples gently making their way down the river.

Something did make him stop dead in his tracks though, whether it was a rustle in the water plants flourishing at the side of the bank, or the indescribable smell that had started to waft up from the hunched form below. It was pitch black at 2am in the morning, the only light coming from the mellow reflection of the moon, part hidden behind the low spring clouds but gently glistening on the almost still surface of the normally tranquil and pleasant river that runs through the sleepy town of Oldcoewood. But Pete did stop and his head turned, and despite being stoned out of his brain he still registered that something wasn't quite right, something was there that shouldn't be there. "Hello?" he called out gingerly, maybe just another drunk bloke at the end of his Friday night out. There was an unwritten competition of the town, that if you drank in Coes Green and lived in Oldcoewood you would run down the hills of the fields as fast as possible to reach the river at the bottom. It was one of those challenges that was mostly suited to fearless kids and crazy drunks as it was almost impossible to stop yourself once you start running. Maybe this guy ran so fast that he couldn't stop himself even when he'd crossed the bridge, and he'd taken the corner too fast, and ended up in the river. That would be a good explanation. That would result in Pete helping the comatose drunk guy up, and them both stumbling out to the main road, laughing at the stupidity of their antics and the drunk guy could either sleep on the park bench by the side of the road, or stumble his way home.

But then why was he almost naked and where were the rest of his clothes? Pete had left his phone at home, but in the poor light of the night sky, he noticed the hunched form was missing most of his attire, and there were no lumps on the bank of the river that might have indicated more belongings. Drunk guy wouldn't have been organised enough to fold his clothes up away from the river before falling in it, and drunk guys generally still have phones in their vicinity. On closer inspection, this guy was literally in a pair of designer pants and nothing else.

Pete took a step closer to the body. "Hey mate." He called out again, there was no answer. One more step towards the river and the hunched over body and Pete could tell there was a problem. "Shit. Fuck…. Oh Jesus Christ" Pete stumbled backwards and fell onto the grass. He was now in a sitting position, staring and what he could most definitely define as a body, not moving in the river. He was now in a situation where he had to do something. He didn't have his phone with him so he couldn't call the police. He cursed himself for always forgetting his phone when he went out at night. Should he move the body out of the river? What if he didn't and it drifted downstream. What if he moved the body but then put his prints all over it? Or what if he moved it and it broke somehow? Did not-moving people break? Snap? After mulling over for more minutes than he wished to, Pete took a few steps forwards towards the body to establish that it was a male, quite a bit older than himself and definitely stuck in the mud.

The scenario made Pete snigger awkwardly as he remembered playing the kids game of Stuck in the Mud, and how no one he ever played with literally WAS stuck in the mud. He knew he shouldn't be laughing but he was still high as a kite and still not sure if he was hallucinating or not. Pete then started to cry, big, ugly sobs. Sobs of confusion about what to do, fear of having found a body in a town where the biggest crime was normally called in from the Supermarket. They had a town meat thief who never quite realised that stealing food from the Tesco Express at the end of the road you live at will always get you into trouble. Everybody knew him and it was a standing joke that they also knew that the CCTV followed him all the way right back to his own front door. A criminal of lesser intelligence and certainly non-threatening variety and a regular focus of entertainment on the previously mentioned local Facebook page.

But this wasn't a local theft, a mugging or a car crash, this was a body, not moving and face down in the river. This is why Pete was crying. He had to get home to report it, and it was amazing how quickly he had put himself into work mode. He had a responsibility, not only as a citizen of Oldcoewood but as the person who ensured that the town was clean and kept it's good countryside town accolade, the town was free of debris, dog shit, rubbish and bodies. And so he ran back home as fast as he could. He would run home, find his phone and call 999 immediately. He reckoned he would be able to report the body within the next 20 minutes if he didn't stop to catch his breath.

Luckily for Pete he didn't have to make it all the way home, as about 8 minutes into his run, which just about got him back onto the street from the fields, and was becoming a struggle, he saw a police car cruising slowly out of the town centre in the direction towards Molville. There was always a little more action going on in Molville on a Friday night, where there were many more pubs and bars than quiet old Oldcoewood . There were no blue lights flashing and Pete just about managed to wave his arms enough to flag the car down. Despite his physical and mental state, it wasn't actually that difficult. He was a highly regarded local, known to everyone as Pete the good guy who cleans up our mess, and here he was weaving on and off the pavement with a panic stricken look across his face and arms flailing everywhere. The car stopped promptly next to him and the windows rolled down for Pete to see PC Carly Cook and PC Daniel Gold inside. Two faces that he recognised immediately, and vice versa. He was extremely relieved and tears started to fall down his sweating cheeks.

"Pete. You alright mate?" asked Carly, immediately recognising one of her local residents.

"I... there... I " Pete was struggling to find the right words to say. He hadn't planned his words, he was still in massive shock and was trying to speak through his sobs. Carly quickly got out of the car to face Pete.

"A body". Pete eventually blurted out "by the river." He inhaled heavily in relief at getting the words out finally.

"What?" Daniel Gold had also now got out of the car and joined Carly, standing opposite Pete by the side of the road. "What are you saying Pete? A body? What do you mean?"

"I.. I was walking over there" Pete pointed in the direction he had just run from. "There's someone in the river. Dead. Not moving. Nothing, no breath" He finally managed to get the words out but the shock of hearing himself say it out loud started off the crying again, and this time it started his body shivering uncontrollably too. Carly walked him over the bench and sat down next to him, a friendly arm around his trembling shoulder.

"Are you saying you've found a dead body?" she asked him as calmly as she could, her own heart beat starting to rise. She wanted to clarify it before she called it in on her radio, hoping that she had misheard what Pete had said, but also partly excited about the drama that could possibly be unfolding.

"Yes" Pete sobbed "I can show you if you want."

He got up and walked back much more slowly this time towards the body he'd found by the bridge in the river. PC's Cook and Gold followed closely behind him, still unsure how much truth there was to what Pete was saying, given his obvious current situation of being totally off his face. They glanced over at one another as they followed, their expressions confirmed that they were both concerned over how out of it Pete actually was. They were not unused to enhanced truths and fabrications, especially on a Friday and Saturday night. They had both come across their equal share of all sorts of amazing stories when they were on the weekend beat and 9 times out of 10, stories are exactly what they were. There were abductions of grown men, who it transpired were actually pissed men who had fallen into bushes and passed out; stories of fatal stabbings where a drunken punch had been thrown and very little damage done, and once even a story of a house being demolished, when it's creator had walked home in completely the wrong direction and ended up in the farm field looking for his three bed semi which wasn't there. But Pete was a trustworthy local, particularly reliable to provide quick and relevant information under any normal circumstances when needed by the two police officers, as he was always out and about, always picking up snippets of other people's conversations and storing them in his mind for later use. The locals liked to stop and tell him what they were up to, and what others were up to. He was neighbourhood watch because the neighbours wanted to connect with him and show their support of what he was doing for the town. They liked that he was known by almost everyone. His facebook posts got many likes and comments. He was overall one of the good guys.

The route back to the river was much easier with a Police standard flashlight and the three of them soon reached the body, which of course hadn't moved in the time Pete had been away from it. With the torch bearing down on him, the body was easily identifiable as a male, no visible signs of breathing and indeed only wearing a pair of boxers. Carly called despatch to get backup.

2.

PC Carly Cook had only been a PC for a year. Prior to that she had spent quite a few years working in the family business, managing the office for her father's haulage firm. She had enjoyed working with her father, but it was never her dream. Despite learning on the job, building the business alongside him and seeing the profits grow to a level that would allow her father to retire whenever he decided to hang his boots up, and overall making her father extremely proud of her in everything she did for the company, she had always dreamed of joining the police force. Carly's mother had passed away five years previously and in the last two years, her father had finally found love again. His new partner couldn't have been more different to Carly's mother, which was quite comforting for Carly, as she could see and treat her as an individual, not a replacement, but realised and appreciated that here was someone who had stepped into her father's life at a time when he was ready to overcome his loss and focus on his future. Carly was now quite convinced that she didn't need to be by his side each and every day. Her brother lived on the other side of London and although they had a close relationship, he hadn't been able to give as much support as Carly had, and she had a responsibility to keep her father occupied, both physically and mentally. But when the time was right, after discussing with him that she was ready to follow her dream, and his blessing for her to do so, alongside profuse apologies for holding her back for so long (which she vehemently denied had anything to do with looking after him), Carly had applied to the force. It was easy for her to get accepted into the force, as she had spent some of her rare free time already as a PCSO, she was addicted to working out and a recognised face in the local gym, and she was a smart, beautiful woman who had just turned 30. An ideal face for the Metropolitan police. From her first day in her induction she hadn't disappointed. Carly breezed through her training with excellent commendations and qualified with top marks to earn her badge.

As a qualified PC, and despite her enthusiasm for the job, Carly didn't want the limelight and 24- hour craziness of London life, with non-stop crime being attested on every street corner. She could have easily made her mark on any of the London units but despite her thirst for the adventure she still felt a duty to stay close to her father and home and was more than happy to join her local force, making her own neighbourhood a safe and secure setting.

For Carly, crime in Oldcoewood was indeed meat thefts from Tesco, drunks outside the pubs mostly at the weekend and rarely violent, lost cats and a few opportunistic van and house burglaries. Nothing unexpected for the town, and she was more than able to accomplish the solving of these crimes in her extremely efficient and polite manner, doing everything she could to minimise future occurrences whilst building strong relationships in the community.

The only dead body she had ever seen was her own mother's, when she had said goodbye to her, in the peaceful and comfortable surroundings of her own bedroom at home. Something that was unfortunately expected and anticipated. Her mother had been ill for a couple of years and had planned her own exit and funeral with the help of the family. It had still been incredibly hard for Carly to accept and not something she would get over in the foreseeable future. But she knew what her mother would have wanted from her, and knew there was little point in putting her life on hold to mourn the loss. Every time Carly went out on her beat, she would glance up at the stars, knowing that she was being looked out for and knowing that her mother would have been just as proud as her father was of her.

And so the shock of seeing a body, lying face down in the river, in her quiet little home town was quite brutal. She too, like Pete had done just a little while before her, stumbled backwards when she saw it. But her professionalism kicked in almost straight away, and she was quick to compose herself, straighten up and put her thinking cap on. 'Do I know this person?' she thought to herself, 'how did he get here?' A barrage of questions was rushing through her mind. 'Woah', she cautioned herself. 'Slow down, one step at a time'. She looked over at her colleague Daniel and could guess that he was thinking the same, and was also in shock. This just didn't happen in Oldcoewood. The last unexplained death was well over 20 years prior when a hitman found and killed his contract in the woods below the newly constructed dual carriageway bridge, that had brought more drama to the town when that was built than the murder itself. It had made national news but then was forgotten by most.

Carly braced herself and calmly called in the find and whilst waiting for back-up, put on her gloves and took a few steps as close to the body as she could, without disturbing the scene.

She could see he was, as Pete had suggested, a white man in his 40's, shaved head probably due to receding hairline, and a bit of a beer belly extended over the waistband of his Hilfiger's. Some stubble on his chin, was that designer or just a lack of shaving? He was also wearing glasses. Simple round frames and lenses. She couldn't see if they were damaged yet, as she didn't want to touch the body before forensics got there. He really just looked like your average guy in town.

She took her flashlight and stepped away from the body to look around the area for any evidence of where he had come from, who he was or any other clues. She and her colleague PC Daniel Gold had been looking for about 15 minutes when the rest of the team turned up. They hadn't found very much at all, other than a few sets of footprints leading up to the river from the direction they had all come in. She knew that her own would be amongst those though, as well as Pete and Daniel. The rest would be for forensics to identify and she would have to be patient to await their findings.

It was approaching 5am by the time Carly and Daniel were able to leave the site and return to the station to start the lengthy processing and writing up their reports. With no clear knowledge of who the corpse belonged to, they would have to wait to see if there were any missing person reports describing him. There was no ID on the body for him to be easily identified, and despite now being Saturday morning, depending on when he had gone missing, there was a low chance of a 40 something male being reported so soon if he had last been seen on Friday night. Carly being Carly however, even though she could quite easily clock off and go home for some sleep whilst the most capable team could pick up where she left off, wanted answers quickly. She couldn't just leave a dead body for others to process. She had a project that she was now destined to see through right to the end.

From what Carly had seen of the mans' face, she thought it slightly familiar, she had an inkling that he was a local and could be identified quickly. It was imperative that she was able to stay on the case, as emotions aside, this would be a huge step up in her career as an officer, but also as a local she knew so many of the residents and knew she would be valuable, especially if the perp was a local too. She didn't want to wait for her DI to come in to work, so she made the decision, despite the hour of the day, to call him and put her case to him.

DI James Sidhu was an understanding officer. He'd been in the Oldcoewood force for almost 20 years now, and held a slight grudge over the much busier station in Molville, where they tended to exert their power, based on the experiences they had even on cases in his jurisdiction. Despite happy leading a more peaceful DI life, he also enjoyed the excitement of the job and welcomed anything out of the ordinary. He was therefore grateful for the call from Carly, and determined to keep the case in his station. When Carly virtually begged him to let her run it, it was a no-brainer that he agreed. She was one of the best officers he'd had come through his ranks and this was the opportunity they had both been waiting for to put themselves on the map.

Carly got off the phone, proud of what she had thought was her best influencing skills, and decided to wait in the office for her boss and the first photographs to come through. She could hold off going home and there was no way she would be able to sleep anyway. It also meant that she could start a local search on social media, friends of friends, local groups. She didn't know why she felt so convinced that he was a local, but she was. And she had always relied on her gut instinct to put her on the right track. Social media, for all it's sins, made the life of a constable so much easier. People loved to share their most precious and private moments with anyone who was bored enough to want to read about them and the force often gained most of their local insight from reading the blue pages of Facebook.

Always the most polite and considerate, she offered everyone in the office a coffee when she went to make her own. The caffeine was going to be necessary.

3.

Cat Ashton woke up far too early for a Saturday morning. It was 6am, yet she hadn't gone to bed before 1am as far as she could remember. She had drunk over a bottle of prosecco to herself, and possibly quite a bit more. She was finding it very hard to remember exactly how much she had drunk, and how she had actually got home too. Her head was already spinning as she reached for the glass of water she tried to keep topped up by the side of her bed, especially for moments like these when she failed to hydrate herself the night before. Thank goodness her two boys were at their Grandparents for the week of the May half term. She was planning to head up to Nottingham, where they were, later that afternoon. She would definitely need to sober up before getting in the car though, and was sure that Billy, her husband wouldn't offer or be in any better state than her to do the honours of driving.

She hated her kids seeing her drunk but felt that she could do very little to prevent it, especially over the past few years. It had become a regular occurrence for them to see her wake up with a hangover from hell, almost weekly, and the week day hangovers she had to hide as best she could, at least until the kids had gone to school and she had a chance to crawl back home for strong black coffee and a cold shower before starting her working day.

This morning Cat felt particularly bad. She had had a tough week, even without having to entertain her children. Her work commitments meant that she had flown to Geneva on the Sunday night, after dropping the kids off at her parent's house and rushing back to drop her car off and catch an Uber to Heathrow with just moments to grab a coffee before boarding the flight. She hadn't returned home until Wednesday evening, despite only packing and preparing for two nights abroad. Her high-profile client, for whom she translated in three different languages, had almost begged her to stay on the extra day, with the promise of a long-term home-based translation project to follow. Cat had been hoping to spend a lot more quality time with her husband Billy during the week whilst the children were away, but the draw of the work and the good money that would come with it took precedence. It was only another 24 hours and she would still have the rest of the week with Billy, and she was sure he wasn't prepared to take time off work to spend with her anyway. She was worried that their marriage was in trouble. Despite working so hard to keep Billy happy, juggling her work and home life to ensure that all his needs were met and the children had what they wanted, she still wasn't sure that she was doing enough and she was scared.

Cat and Billy had met 14 years prior at a mutual friend's wedding. They had hit it off instantly and shared a couple of bottles of champagne between them as they got to know one another and flirted on the dancefloor. The evening had ended with a kiss and the swapping of phone numbers. Cat had gone back to her own flat in central London and Billy back to his in Oldcoewood. Cat, showing her strong independent personality had called him the next afternoon and Billy had been pleased to hear from her. The relationship blossomed quickly, as Billy worked in London and found it easy to spend nights with Cat when he had been out drinking with his workmates and didn't quite fancy the last tube home, only to be back on it at 7am the following morning. Cat was happy with the attention and the late night company, and it also hadn't passed her by that Billy came from good stock, he was well spoken and well educated. His job in insurance sounded important to Cat and he always made a point of putting his card behind the bar on a night out, ate in fancy restaurants and she liked that he chose her menu options for her. Wasn't that a sign of affluence?

Cat had moved down to London from her family home in Nottingham after finishing her degree in languages. Whilst studying, she had taken additional elocution lessons to give herself more of a home -counties accent and was proud of her personal achievement in becoming a self-employed translator. She looked back at her friends who had either become teachers or secretaries and knew that she was on to bigger and better things. She was excited that her job took her to many interesting parts of the world, and she had made sure to invest in the best travel luggage to show her fellow travellers that she had those luxuries usually assigned to first class voyagers. Alas she was still however travelling economy class, but she had plans. Plans to become rich and marry well and live more of a princess style life. When Billy came on to the scene, it looked like he would suit her plans very well. Her mother couldn't quite understand where this longing for such affluence had come from, as they had always been a very happy family in their modest family home. They had afforded holiday's abroad during Cat and her sister's childhood but it had never seemed enough for Cat who, as a youngster, drooled over the pages of Hello magazine and would watch Dynasty over Coronation Street and Beverley Hills 90210 over Grange Hill every time.

Cat and Billy dated for three years before Cat fell pregnant with their first son, Ned. They still had their separate homes at the time and it was only then that she put a little pressure on Billy for them to move in together. Her flat in London was rented and Billy wanted to live closer to his family and so they decided to stay in Oldcoewood, putting all their savings together to buy their soon-to-be family home. It was a lovely 3- bedroom semi-detached house in a nice area of Oldcoewood, close to some very good schools and only a mile from the station. Billy took control of the mortgage and Cat assumed that he would get them the best deal, considering the deposit covered a decent chunk of the price.

Of course, living in Oldcoewood together meant that Billy would have to make sure he got the last train home from London when he was out drinking, or forfeit the £60 taxi fare. Occasionally he would stay over with a colleague who lived more centrally and Cat did notice that he was gradually cutting back on his nights out, although he would always defend the ones that he did go on, and the dent it made to his wallet. "It is all networking" he would reassure her. "When you're in my kind of role, it's important to be known amongst clients and competitors alike.   My best business is done after a few bottles and a decent curry".

Cat didn't really mind. She was overwhelmed with her pregnancy and that she was in a happy and stable relationship with the love of her life. She was excited that they had bought their starter home together. She anticipated two or three years in this house before they would move onwards and upwards to her forever home with spare rooms for visitors, bathrooms en-suite and a garden that would certainly require a regular gardener.

That was 11 years ago, and during that 11 years she had given birth to Ned and then two years later Jason had come along. Two beautiful healthy boys with their dad's eyes and her blonde hair. She and Billy got married a year after Jason was born and they were still living in the same house, which deep down she did quite love and was extremely fond of, but Cat often thought about her forever house, waiting patiently for her to buy. She was sure it would happen and prayed that it would be sooner rather than later. Soon enough for her school-mum friends to admire and be envious of. Ned was now in the last year of primary school and she had worked very hard to secure a close-knit group of friends with similar interests to her own. Predominantly money and drinking. She was constantly aware of the luxuries they had and where she needed to up her game and where necessary, compete to impress. It was in her nature to always try and influence her audience, show them what she wanted them to think she was made of. She would never sit back and allow others to govern her status. She always put on an excellent show and was very convincing.

Deep down though, her relationship with Billy was really rocky. She knew that she was a great wife and mother, having taken a year off after both births to look after her babies and provide an almost Stepford wives home for Billy. She continued to be a great mother and wife after she went back to work and would make sure, even when she had been out to a client, whether in London or elsewhere in the country, that she would make a freshly home cooked meal, pandering to both the boys' fussy childish needs and Billy's demanding gourmet needs. She was tired at the end of a long day, and sometimes she didn't quite do it right, but desperately hoping that her effort would suffice and be recognised. However, if Billy was in a bad mood, and tired himself, if it wasn't up to his standard he would refuse to eat what she had cooked, instead throwing it straight in the bin and ordering himself a takeaway. Occasionally, when she had cooked a superb offering, he might not have gotten home until 2am, by which time, of course, a microwaved version of the effort and thought that had gone into the previous meal didn't have the desired effect.

The good news was that Billy did now spend less time drinking in London, now that he had his new crew locally too. Cat knew that she had influenced this and was proud of the hard work that had come to fruition.

A part of Cat's life plan was to put her children in the best local school that she could without having to pay for it, and she happily found that she was abundant in the choice of school's locally. Once she had got Ned into reception, she had sat down with Billy and analysed every single other parent in the class. Which of them had the biggest houses, who had the best jobs and the nicest cars? There's no denying that Cat was materialistic, but her motto had always been, you don't become a millionaire unless you think like a millionaire and act like one too. The mums were generally all very friendly and the kids were all adorable too, but Cat had worked out the ones who would benefit her and those who didn't need the energy wasted on them. Billy hadn't taken much interest in her analytics. He was too busy being Billy and doing whatever the hell he wanted to do.

It took about a year for her to finalise her plan, and then she was delighted to find that a number of her chosen clique also had kids the same age as Jason. This was a major achievement in her life plan and she made sure that to ensure its continuation Billy would arrange nights out with the chosen dads too. The clique husbands had been well sourced by Cat, and she was happy that Billy could form local friendships with these guys in high places. There was no point in having a wealthy friend with a dull husband that Billy would just ignore if he was in the mood. that could have a knock-on effect on other parents and their views of her sometimes unpredictable husband. Also, by having good local friends, who also partied like her husband, she had more control over where Billy was when he went out drinking, and she knew she could depend on the other mums to keep her entertained too. A long-term investment in her future lifestyle did mean a lot more prosecco and wine, and her savings were becoming less and less each month as her social life slowly expanded. She was happy though. She was slowly creating her dream and it was all falling into place.

However, as Billy moved up in the world of insurance and Cat was bogged down in her triple life of mum, worker and social butterfly, Billy looked more to his buddies for entertainment and to his wife for housekeeping. When she suggested some time away just the two of them, he booked rugby tickets for the lads. When she said she'd booked a restaurant for them whilst the kids were away, he said he would be late home. When she asked him if he loved her, he just smiled and kissed the top of her head. She felt she was becoming a Nancy to his Bill Sykes. To those on the outside they were a fantastic, fun-loving beautiful couple. The reality was at home, she was really miserable, very lonely and constantly worried about what Billy would do next.

When he was drunk he loved her, when he was drunk he came home very raunchy, waking her up for quick, messy and painful sex that she found hard to enjoy. In fact he was spending less and less time with her sober and to compensate, she was also spending less and less time sober, but they weren't drinking together, only when the group allowed for it and there was a party, or when it was one of the kids birthdays and they arranged a party at home for the kids in their clique so that the parents could stay too and the prosecco and beer could flow from early afternoon until early morning.

During this half term week, and whilst she was sitting alone in her hotel room in Geneva, Cat had had a lot of time to think. She needed to work on her marriage and rekindle the love between herself and Billy. She really did love Billy and couldn't think of a life with them apart. Aside from being massively jealous should he ever have another woman in his life, and equally jealous of the relationship he would have with the children, she did think there was something to fight for. She didn't want to be a divorcee. She wanted her and Billy to love each other right until the end, like her parents were doing. She called him from Geneva and told him she was booking a restaurant for Wednesday night and he had to be there. He reluctantly agreed, Wednesday's were quiet drinking days generally so he could afford to spend some time with his wife. Even Billy thought that he hadn't seen much of her over the past few weeks, so he could try and make more of an effort.

Cat returned home, got an Uber back to their house and unpacked her case, putting a load of washing in the machine, as she noticed that Billy hadn't done any whilst she was away. She showered and changed and spent a little time on her hair and makeup before it was time to go out. They stayed local and went to the new Italian restaurant in the high street. That way they could walk home afterwards and not worry about spending unnecessarily on cabs.

The evening didn't go quite as planned for Cat. They went to the restaurant and Billy ordered the drinks straight away. He then proceeded to flirt with the waitress throughout the evening, to the point where the waitress asked one of her male colleagues to take over as she was getting highly embarrassed by his behaviour. That angered Billy and started him off on a vindictive bashing of Cat about everything and anything he could think of. She tried on numerous occasions to defend herself but her words fell on deaf ears, and eventually she gave up trying and focussed on drinking to keep up with him. She couldn't recall what the food tasted like by the end of their evening. And when they left the restaurant it started to rain. Billy walked in front of Cat with his umbrella covering his shaved head and she scuttled behind trying to keep up and trying to make polite conversation. There was no sex that night, neither romantic nor drunken, and Thursday morning Billy had already left for work when Cat woke up. She hated failure, and so she decided to try again Thursday evening with a home cooked meal and less alcohol. But Billy came home from work around 9pm that night and Cat literally threw his dinner at him before taking herself off to bed for an early night. On Friday, Billy was working from home and so they sat and had breakfast together. A pleasant chat about the kids activities with their grandparents that week, and how the weather was great up there for them being outdoors so much. She was feeling confident again and believed that their last night without the kids could be the one that she had hoped for all week. Billy then declared that he was going out with the boys that night but would eat before he went out. Cat's heart sank and she couldn't hide her disappointment. Cat hadn't arranged to go out with the girls, and she knew at least two of them were visiting family out of the area. She didn't want to be left on her own again and so made the most of the day time to plan her own evening at short notice.

She made a few calls but none of her usual posse were around and so she looked further afield to some of the other mums with boys in Ned's class. Not quite her elite crowd but actually they were nice girls and a good laugh. She was in luck as three of them were planning to go to the pub anyway and she was welcome to join them.

And that is how Friday evening started. After a quick and simple pasta meal, Cat and Billy both went to the Dog and Duck pub but once there found their separate groups and left one another. The men were being very loud and very lechy, but Cat had to turn a blind eye and focus on the women she was with and whose round it was for the Prosecco. At some point Billy's lot left the pub, by then she had no idea what time it was or whether he had bothered to come and say goodbye to her. She was far too drunk to notice or even really care.

And now it was 6am on Saturday morning, she turned to see if Billy was lying next to her in their bed, he wasn't. She gradually made her way out of their room and into the boys' rooms to see if he had made it to either of their beds. They were both empty too and so she went back into her room, put on her dressing gown and went downstairs. Billy wasn't on the sofa either, his keys weren't on the key plaque in the kitchen and thankfully his car was still in the driveway. At least he hadn't done anything stupid like coming home to drive off somewhere.

She would call the other guys later in the morning, he must have gone home with either Richard or Lee who lived nearer to the town centre.

4.

Billy hadn't gone back to either Richard or Lee's houses that Friday night, because he was indeed lying on the bank of the river about a mile and a half away from their homes. Cat had waited until late morning to try and locate her husband. Worst case scenario, if they boys had had a really late night/early morning, she would still expect them to have woken up by 11am. They weren't students any more. She didn't have Richard's number stored on her phone and so she called his wife and one of her best friend's Natalya. Even though Natalya had told Cat she was going away for the weekend, and therefore wasn't part of her proposed outing on the Friday night, she could at least give Cat Richard's number or give him a call herself.

Natalya answered the phone after just a couple of rings. She sounded quite drowsy. "You sound like you've had a good night out then!" Cat greeted her.

"Oh hi Cat" Natalya almost slurred her words. "What's up?"

"Oh I just wondered if you could give Richard a call for me please and see if Billy ended up on your couch last night, he's not come home yet."

"No, he's not here" Natalya answered too promptly.

"I thought you were away this weekend?" Cat's tone of voice changed to an accusing one. She immediately started to think of all the reasons why her friend had lied to her. Thoughts of her husband went out of her head and she was fuming. The one thing Cat hated more than anything was not to be a part of any news being shared. "I had to go out with the other lot, you know, the football mum's rather than us Rugby ones" she snapped. "Still had a good night though, but why didn't you say you were home?" She was desperately trying to calm her voice to sound cool and nonchalant.

"Sorry, I told you I was going away. It's nothing important though " said Natalya, "but as you now know I didn't actually go away, I'm not feeling very well"

"You should have said!" Cat chirped up suddenly. She was always looking to help out her friends. She needed to be needed, and she needed to constantly be in their line of sight, even if that meant offering to do the odd chore for them, or taking their kids more regularly than they might take hers. She sometimes did wonder if she was a bit of a doormat, but she was prepared to take that label, if it meant she was at the forefront of what was going on.

A voice boomed in the background of the phone call. It was Richard, laughing and shouting out something that Cat couldn't hear. "Fucking just shut it" Cat heard Natalya whisper angrily at her husband.

"What was that all about?" Cat exclaimed. "

"Oh Richard's just being a jerk, ignore him" Natalya quickly responded. "Anyway, I'm lying ill on the sofa and have been for most of the weekend. So I know that Billy hasn't been here, otherwise he'd be on the sofa with me right now." Natalya continued, almost chuckling. "Have you asked Lee? Oh hang on, Richard says Billy didn't walk home with them but he can't quite remember when they parted company. Ha ha he's probably pissed up lying in a gutter somewhere. You'll have to send out a search party!"

Cat laughed and said her goodbyes. She got off the phone and sat for a moment, thinking where else he might have gone. She was quite pleased that he hadn't gone to Richard's though, as Natalya, she thought, was always a little too flirty with her husband. They were all part of a close group of friends, a group that she had carefully constructed herself, and she was happy with the group. Happy with the relationships between all of them, husbands, wives and kids together, but she had noticed on a number of occasions Natalya placing her hand a little too long on Billy's thigh, or fluttering her eyelids at him and giggling at literally all of his jokes, even the really lame ones. Cat had put that down a lot to her being drunk and a naturally flirty character. She had had her suspicions about the pair of them but didn't want to believe her own thoughts, so she convinced herself there was nothing going on, and when she noticed Natalya flirting with Bill, she tried her hardest to equally flirt with Richard, despite there being no attraction to him whatsoever. And Natalya and Richard had a good solid relationship anyway. Richard was very successful and had just completed a huge overhaul project at his recruitment company, lots of changes and new processes which had lead to a massive increase in clients, which meant that they would soon be rolling in it, and most probably upgrade their modest 3 bed semi for a bigger detached mansion with spare rooms and knowing them a pool that wouldn't be used for the best part of the year.

And to top that off, Natalya loved money more than anything. She wouldn't swap her soon to be millionaire husband for a meagre Insurance salesman that Billy was. Cat was annoyed with herself for constantly overthinking things. But deep down she did know and was in no position to admit it to herself. She wasn't stupid, and she certainly wasn't naive but she had seen the time when Billy and Natalya both disappeared for about 20 minutes at one of the many house parties their clique held. It hadn't been just a coincidence, them both disappearing at the same time, but she had told herself and desperately tried to convince herself at the time that she had been so hammered that it was more likely herself who had disappeared and fell asleep in a corner of the living room or something. And that had been ages ago, she hadn't noticed anything like that for a while. Surely she had nothing to worry about.

Except the whereabouts of her husband right now.

Simultaneously, Natalya was lying back on the couch at home, high on the painkillers her specialist had given her, also thinking about the whereabouts of Cat's husband. It was only a few months ago that she and Billy had found themselves in a very compromising position at Jaycee and Simon's house. Just a regular evening with copious amounts of prosecco and beer, a few random cocktails designed by Wayne and his flamboyant alcoholic ideas and a very short T-shirt dress worn by Natalya, that one might mistaken think had been taken straight out of the wardrobe of her 12 year old daughter. She was convinced that she had the same body as her almost teen, much bigger boobs of course, but the ability to wear whatever she liked, and however she liked to. Unlike her daughter though, she wouldn't be seen dead shopping in Primark, and her own wardrobe was a no go area for her daughter. everything in it was far too designer. Being in her 40s was not going to be a barrier to her looking as good as she could. She just hoped that she wouldn't resent her friends as they started to look and dress more their own ages, she didn't want them to let her aesthetic down.

Natalya had been absolutely hammered, to the point where her recollection of a big chunk of the evening was a complete blur. She remembered having a deep conversation at one point with Jaycee about the tiles on her kitchen splashback but then she had no idea why she left the conversation and followed Billy out into the expansive hallway, with its over the top golden chandelier hanging down over the grand front entrance in the house.

This was a house she really admired, and she was basing her aspiration and dream for her own next home on this. Not her tiny three bed semi, just a road away from Billy and Cat. That was just an interim move whilst they were waiting for the big shit to kick off. She wouldn't admit to anyone else that they lived on the wrong side of the main residential street of Oldcoewood, the more modest side with far too many council houses for her liking. Not that she didn't like the people who lived there, she did actually like quite a few of them, her kids had friends nearby and some of the other mums were nice enough, and useful enough too when she couldn't be bothered to chauffeur them from one club to another. She rarely returned the favour, it just wasn't in her best interest to get involved with other people's children, or to be helpful. She had only agreed to move to her current house because Richard had wanted to release some money from their previous large house in Molville, to put into building his recruitment consultancy, and had spent a very long time convincing her, showing her the business forecast and everything else he could think of to get her buy-in before she eventually agreed. And thank god it had finally come to fruition. Natalya was absolutely ready to move into her forever home, with many more rooms than she needed and a kitchen with cupboards that would never be full because there were so many of them. And of course a chandelier, bigger and grander than Jaycee's.

And so Natalya vaguely recalled standing in the hallway with the reflection from the lights shining on her highlighted hair and Billy had said something to her, she had no idea what it actually was, but it had made her follow him into the downstairs cloakroom. This wasn't a toilet but the old style portrayal of a room just for coats and boots with an uncomfortable but stylish wooden bench against the wall. Billy had mentioned to Natalya earlier in the evening that he was enjoying the view of her child's dress and made some smarmy comment about whether she had kids knickers on underneath it. This dress had actually cost Natalya a small fortune and certainly didn't come out of her daughter's wardrobe, and so she was glad that it was drawing attention, even if only from her friends' husband. But how could she have no recollection of exactly what happened in the cloakroom. Natalya wasn't that stupid that she couldn't work it out, but she really didn't remember either having full sex with Billy or whether it was a quick blow job from her part and a groping fingering from him. Either way Billy had left her in the room afterwards when he went back into the lounge to continue his drinking and to talk Rugby with the lads as if nothing at all had happened.

Natalya had literally pulled her knickers up and adjusted her dress back into place, smoothed down her hair and headed back into the kitchen to find a couple of the girls topping up their prosecco glasses. She didn't dare look over at Cat but she quickly found her glass again and rejoined the group without anyone questioning her whereabouts.

Since that night, Billy had been texting her with requests and demands of what he would like to do to her next. She only had one mobile phone, as being a stay at home mum meant she had no requirement for a work phone and prior to this had nothing to hide. But now she was petrified that Richard would stumble across these texts should he pick up her phone for some reason or other. She had replied to Billy not to text her and never to mention this again. He had replied with a laughing emoji and an aubergine, how uncouth she thought. She replied again, this time more seriously. Billy, if you text me again on this number I literally will kill you. Don't ruin my marriage, don't be so fuckng petty. Stop this IMMEDIATELY. For Billy it was an empty threat, and it didn't work. He continued to text her with his suggestions and requests, and bored Natalya, knowing she should have just deleted them, or blocked Billy, read each one of them, until she gave in to him and they started to find times when they could meet up for sex. Sex in the car, sex in her friend's bed, even sex in the toilets at his office one evening when most of the company had gone home and he demanded her to get the train in to London. She had told Richard that she had to go and see one of her many consultants. Richard was so used to her seeing different specialists for different parts of her ever changing body that he didn't think twice about it. This had been going on now for a couple of months although always on Billy's terms.

She had seen Billy just a week ago when they went round to Billy and Cat's for a takeaway and a few drinks of course, and she found it very hard to make any eye contact with him all evening. She was really concerned that Cat or Richard would notice something going on, and wanted to act as normal as she possibly could, and so she forced herself to be ever so slightly flirty, as she always was with the men, but that night she wasn't at all happy with Billy's positive response to her flirting, and his hand on her arm more often than she liked, his constant staring at her cleavage with raised eyebrows. How the hell did Cat deal with his constant roaming eye? At least she was wearing jeans tonight, and they were so tight, there was no way they were coming down until she was ready to climb into bed with her own husband. Deep down she was ashamed of what she and Billy had done, ashamed that she had betrayed her friend and her own husband. She was planning on ending the affair anyway. Put it in the past and forget all about it. It was time for her to focus on love from her husband and visual attention only from all the other men.

And now where was Billy? Had he found some other silly bitch to abuse whilst he was out, and gone back to her house whilst her husband wasn't aware and poor Cat was home alone? Well it wasn't Natalya's problem, and there was very little she could do about it anyway, she had to worry about the bruising that was making an awesome appearance on her legs in bold colours of yellow and purple and wondering whether it was too soon for more painkillers with her strong black coffee for breakfast.

5.

Lee had no knowledge of the whereabouts of Billy either. When Cat called him (as she did actually have his phone number saved on her phone), he told her that he had walked home with Richard, but Billy had said goodbye in the pub. He thought he'd gone back in to use the Loo or to speak to someone else. Lee had had to leave the pub in an emergency so that he could throw up in the bush around the corner without being seen. Tequila was not his favourite shot at all, and never agreed with him, and he never understood why he always gave in to drinking it when he was out. Lee's wife Marie was indeed away with her mum and the kids for the weekend in their holiday home in Great Yarmouth. Despite loving spending time with his family, he did also enjoy that freedom and very rare pretence that he was a singleton again. not for the women or the flirting but for the late nights, the heavy drinking and no one to tell him that he shouldn't be sleeping on the sofa or cooking bacon sarnies at 2am. Lee had stumbled home, with absolutely no knowledge of the time or the route he took, but there was just him and the cat in the house, and he wasn't even sure if the cat was there.

Lee stayed on the phone with Cat whilst he looked around his surroundings. He had crawled downstairs from his bedroom to find a few empty packets of crisps and half a glass of water on the kitchen island. So he didn't quite make it to an early breakfast when he got in, but there was definitely no sign of any other person being in the property, which was also a good sign, as cautious Lee had forgotten to double lock the front door too.

Cat really liked Lee. He was a genuine, kind guy, who obviously adored his wife Marie, and was also an amazing cook. When they had evenings at their house, Lee would always cook up something interesting, spicy and unique to go with the many drinks that formed the basis of their evenings. He even did the washing up after his cooking and Cat had noticed on more than one occasion there were fresh flowers on the dining room table that Marie hadn't bought herself.

In fact, Cat was quite jealous of the relationship that Lee and Marie had. Their kids were also very polite and well behaved, where hers were turning into mini versions of their father, demanding food when they knew she was busy working, and walking away whenever she asked them to tidy up after themselves. Lee and Marie had the ideal relationship that she so wanted with Billy, and she spent hours and hours trying to recreate it in her own home. She loved going round to Marie's house and subtly ask questions about Marie and Lee's relationship, how much Marie had to do around the house to keep her man happy, if she really just had to ask her boys to tidy their rooms and they did, how she got on so well with her husband and what they chatted about over dinner each evening. Deep down Cat was desperately trying to see if this was all just a surface act, and there was actually a whole different scenario hidden from sight, behind closed doors that would satisfy her need to know that no one had it good in reality and happy homes were just a visual for insta posts.

But every time she asked Marie about her home life, she got very similar answers. She was deliriously happy. She worked part time as a nursery teacher, and sometimes when she was tired she would tell Lee to do the cooking or order in a curry. They even sometimes did the supermarket shop together, although that would often mean over spending as Lee would want to experiment with new world foods that she had no idea how to cook. She talked about Lee's moods. If he'd had a bad day at work they would sit down and talk about it and she would make him feel better, but he did exactly the same for her if she needed it too. Marie was the boss of the household, and had no problem at all in taking charge of each day.

Marie had blushed when Cat had asked about her sex life. She often talked of times when Lee worked from home, and she couldn't even have a shower on her own without him interrupting her, just because the kids were at school and the cat was out somewhere being fed by their neighbours, sitting on somebody else's sofa watching This Morning. Cat tried and tried but couldn't find any dirt at all, so she finally resigned herself to admiring their lives and fighting off the jealousy instead of doing everything she could to make her own life more like Marie's. Deep down she was bitterly jealous. One day, she thought, one day something will come to light and she could say to herself "I told you so!"

Lee and Cat chatted on the phone a while longer, trying to establish who else Billy had spoken to in the pub, what his mood was, and who else was around. It was pretty much a pointless exercise though as Lee had been so drunk he could barely remember a thing. "I think at one point when Billy went to the bar, he was chatting to a guy whose son goes to Rugby. I can't remember his name though, or even the son's. To be honest Cat, I wasn't really paying attention, Sky Sports news was on in the background and I was trying to focus on the ticker bar until I couldn't read any of the words any more. He'll be home soon, I'm sure though."

Cat murmured an agreement and hung up.

If he hadn't come home with Lee or Richard, who the hell had he gone home with? She tried his mobile a few more times but it just rang out. It wasn't switched off though and she couldn't work out if that was a good sign or not!

6.

DI Sidhu had rushed into the station and was greeted with a fresh coffee that Carly had preempted and brought in for him. She brought him up to date on her findings and asked for his approval for her to continue with what she was doing. DI Sidhu agreed, he was happy with her attention to detail and the processes she was putting in place. He had a lot of faith in this young PC and could see her rising up the ranks in good time.

Carly was waiting for forensics to come back with fingerprints taken from the scene, and for the photographs of the dead body to develop. When they came through later that Saturday morning, it took her only a few minutes to identify Billy Ashton, local man, father of two and Rugby coach for the local kids team. They had also managed to find a wallet, hidden in the bush about 10 feet away from where the body was found. The wallet contained a driving licence confirming its' owner was William Andrew Ashton, a credit card with the same name, and a twenty pound note. Of course they would still need to match the DNA but there was very little doubt. No one had called in the missing person yet, but then it was still quite early on a Saturday morning for someone to either realise that he was missing or really be that concerned that a grown 40 something man had been gone for just one night.

"Sir, do you mind if I go home and freshen up?" Carly asked her boss. "I think I'm starting to stink the whole station out" she blushed. Sidhu nodded and laughed as he pinched his nose "Go on, you'd best go quickly" he joked "before people start to talk. When you're refreshed do you want to come with me to tell the family?" his face straightened as he got back to thinking about the job. "Yes please sir" Carly was quick to reply. "I would really welcome that opportunity."

"Fine, I'll pick you up at 10" was the reply as Carly made her way out of the door. That gave Carly a little more time to collect her dog from her neighbour on the way home and still get some breakfast and a shower in. By the time DI Sidhu was outside her house, she felt a lot better and smelt a lot fresher. The journey to the Ashton house was a relatively quiet one and it gave Carly time to rehearse her part of the speech over and over. She'd never had to tell anyone before of a body that had been discovered. She didn't want to sound like she was in a movie, or some corny cop drama, but actually, there is only one way to communicate such news. DI Sidhu had given her leeway to start off the conversation. Previously whenever she had been out with PC Gold, she had let him do most of the talking, albeit on the side of making arrests rather than portraying such awful news. Daniel had opted to go home and freshen up himself but arranged to meet up with Carly later at the station to start analysing the information they were quickly collecting.

Daniel also preferred the quiet town of Oldcoewood to his previous area of Tower Hamlets. He had spent a few years patrolling East London and had come across his fair share of bodies, mostly related to drugs or gangs, and despite years of trying to change views and habits, it had got all a bit too much for him, and he knew that if he ever got bored or homesick, he could just take a trip into Molville on a Saturday night, especially after a home football game to remind himself why he left the lights of the big city behind. Although he loved his job, he loved his family more and the comfort in returning home to them every evening in one piece kept him happy in the sleepy town with little drama.

DI Sidhu and Carly were on their way to Billy's house as the streets were starting to wake up and kids were running out of front doors, in their sports gear, footballs under arms, swimming bags over shoulders. Dogs out on leads, hopefully their owners kitted out with enough bags to clean up their own dog's shit and not leave it for some poor kid to skid through in the park. Billy Ashton's road was quiet, a nice residential cul de sac of neat and tidy three bed semi's and a small block of maisonettes on the bend. Quite decent cars in the driveways, Carly noticed that virtually all of them had 4 wheels, windows and hub caps. Nothing was missing or damaged on them. She'd seen a few roads locally where driveways were being used as mechanic's garages and bits of cars lay all over the lawns, some spilling out on the pavement. She didn't like that. She was a bit OCD when it came to appearances and layout of the expected. Front gardens should have a drive and a little bit of lawn, back gardens should have lawn and a little bit of paving. Houses should look symmetrical, windows either side of the front door and that kind of thing. It meant to Carly that even if things weren't right behind the wooden doors, they looked the part from the road. Billy Ashton's house didn't disappoint. It looked like a proper neat little house and she immediately liked it. Not that she would ever say anything if she didn't. She wasn't one to force her personal opinion on others, having witnessed it far too many times where locals would mouth off about their neighbours, how they didn't like the way they'd painted the window frames, or hadn't mowed their lawns. there were a lot of strong opinions in the neighbourhood and she didn't care for a single one of them. Each to their own, she often thought. She knew what she liked but was happy for everyone else to do what the hell they liked, as long as they weren't breaking the law.

Carly and her boss walked up the driveway and knocked at the front door. The house seemed quiet considering Billy had two young sons. They waited just a few short moments before Cat Ashton answered the door. A pleasant looking woman, she was dressed simply in jeans and a plain T-shirt. She wasn't wearing make-up and she'd obviously not spent any time on her hair as yet this early on a Saturday morning.

Cat did a double take at the two police officers standing on her doorstep. This couldn't be connected to Billy going missing, could it? It must be a coincidence. She looked them up and down, and looked again.

Finally the female police officer spoke. "Mrs Ashton?" she asked. Cat nodded. Confused, bemused. She looked up and down the road, looking for other police officers outside other houses, carrying out routine visits. Looking for a clue other than the obvious one staring her right in the face. "I'm Police Constable Carly Cook, and this is Detective Inspector James Sidhu" she continued. "Can we come in please?"

Can we come in? Cat thought. That's not door to door inquiries into a regular street incident, or a follow up of some anti-social behaviour. Police came in because you're in trouble. She hesitated but quickly corrected herself and took a step back to open the door wider. "Yes, please do, " she said. She led the way through the hall and into the kitchen. Cat's mind was in overload and she almost giggled as she thought to herself how funny it was that most activities are carried out in the kitchen and no one uses their lounges any more aside from TV watching and flopping into sofa's at the end of a long day. Kitchens are the hub of most houses, and the current trend for kitchen Islands and kitchen stools makes that even more possible. Cat was proud that the one room she had managed to refurbish was indeed her kitchen, with it's clean, cream gloss finish and bi-folding doors spanning the width of the house. And so that is where she led the two police officers. Into her kitchen and seated on bar stools at the island. She offered them coffee or tea, but both declined. She knew she was waffling, but it was what she did when she was nervous and worried. She had run out of ideas now for the purpose of the visit. It was time for them to do the talking.

"Mrs Ashton" Carly started. "You might want to sit down yourself". She paused,indicating towards the empty stool by the island and waited, at the same time listening for sounds of anyone else in the house or any other movement. When she was convinced there was no one coming into the room she continued, "I'm so sorry to do this, but early this morning, a body was found in the river Ketch. We think it may be your husband, Billy Ashton".

Cat turned white, she slid back in her seat, almost falling off the high stool onto the cold tiles below. "What?... How?" There were no words to decipher the mess of thoughts going through her head.

Carly got up and immediately fetched her a glass of water, rinsing out a glass she found on the draining board. She was sure it still had flecks of juice in it, but timing was important and she didn't want to spend too long either searching for another glass or cleaning this one out completely. Cat took the glass off Carly without acknowledging it. She was staring ahead into space, barely breathing as she took in the news that she had just been exposed to.

DI Sidhu was in no denial they had the right person and as he looked over at Carly, she acknowledged that the next stage was all admin as they now had to get official confirmation and sign paperwork. Why was there always so much paperwork involved with living and dying? Everything needed a stamp on it, a signature, an authority, when really it was so blatantly obvious. She was sitting with a woman who had just been told that her husband had been found dead and her next question would be to ask this poor woman to come and physically identify the body and sign a piece of paper to say that indeed, it was her husband lying in a morgue. She took a step towards the now shivering woman and put her arm around Cat as she explained how they had found him, the time, the place. Cat didn't change her expression or move her face to respond to Carly but she could hear every word sinking into her brain, smothering every other thought. "We fish in that river with the boys," she finally whispered.

James asked where the boys were and Cat managed to tell him they were with their grandparents for the weekend. She was home alone.

Half an hour later, Cat, James and Carly were walking into the morgue at the local hospital. Cat had insisted on doing her hair and make-up before leaving the house. She had no idea why, but knew she couldn't go there without having done so. Billy had never liked her to be anything less than fully made up, he told her that it made her look like she didn't care about their relationship if she couldn't look her best when she was with him. Even when she was lying in bed with the flu, she had still managed to put a little mascara on to keep him happy.

The journey in the police car had been quiet, no one spoke to one another. There were a few pleasantries from the two police officers with the staff in the hospital and then they made their way down to the morgue.

It was very cold down there and Cat almost wished she'd brought her new wool coat that she'd treated herself to for her birthday, pretending that it had come from Billy and the kids. When she saw the body lying on the slab she gasped and immediately reached out to grab James who was standing next to her. Then she wept. Her husband was lying dead on the table in front of her. He had bruising around his neck and his face was bloated, presumably from all the water he'd consumed in the river. But there was no denying it was her husband.

"That's Billy" she whispered, not taking her eyes off the body. The words coming out of her mouth were like a release. Her shoulders dropped, she breathed in and out deep breaths, not the shallow, short breaths that hit her back at the house. "That's Billy" she said again, a little louder this time, concerned that she hadn't been heard the first time. Of course she had. All eyes were on her as she identified her husband lying there.

in response to her confirmation, Carly took her by her shoulders and gently steered her away from the body. "Thank you" she said quietly. "We can leave now and take you back home". But Cat was transfixed. How could her husband, whom she only saw the evening previously as they were getting ready to go out their separate ways, be lying there dead now. It had been less than 24 hours. The last thing she had said to him was "Don't drink more than me", and the last thing he had said to her was "Don't wait up" and now they would never have a conversation again. Never argue, never fight, never make love, never hold hands and the children would never see their dad again. How could life change so dramatically, so quickly? It was impossible. "What happens now?" she whispered as she was being led out of the room. Carly explained that they would have to do an autopsy, but that might take a day or two. Cat would be updated on the that and the outcome, and then they could release the body for a funeral whilst they continued their investigation into his death.

Carly told her boss that she would go back to the house with Cat, so they could start to put a plan together on how she would inform her family, his family, their friends. She advised Cat not to be alone for the day, but also not to get the children back a day early. Cat now had to project manage her own husband's death. He was always causing her work to do, he was always the centre of attention and this hadn't even changed now that he was lying on a cold white slab, grey in colour and not breathing.

She bit her lip as she went to find a pen and some paper to write on. Carly offered to make some of the calls for her, but she declined. This was her husband, her responsibility. She called her own mother first, thinking it would be easier than Billy's parents.

Within the hour, Cat had notified both sets of parents and had called Natalya, knowing that she was at home and could let everyone else know. She hadn't cried during any of the phone calls. She was miles outside of her own body and could almost visualise herself sitting on the couch, searching her contacts for the right people to call. She would have to email his boss on Monday. Maybe she'd let the police do that one. She didn't know Billy's boss, even though he'd worked for the same company and in the same department for over 6 years. She'd never gone to any of his work Christmas parties or gatherings. There had been plenty of these each year, but she was always told partners were not invited. She didn't know any of Billy's colleagues to verify that either. It was a completely separate life he led away from his family one in Oldcoewood. Yes, she was certain that she would pass over that one to the police.

During her call with Natalya, Cat has asked if she was around to pop in and give the Police woman a break, but Natalya had declined much to Cat's surprise. She gave the excuse that she was still feeling very ill and didn't want to pass on anything she might have. She hadn't sounded ill when she answered the phone, but her voice seemed to get worse throughout the conversation. Natalya told Cat that she would send Richard over straight away instead. Confused and annoyed by her friend, Cat reluctantly agreed and Richard was soon joined by Lee and the two of them sat awkwardly on the couch with Cat, desperately trying to think of something to say, other than "how did that happen?" and "Oh my God I'm so sorry Cat". They weren't much help, and very little comfort. Cat almost felt more sorry for them than herself, they were full of self pity for the loss of their friend, providing no real comfort for her in this horrific situation. And so after a couple of hours of sitting awkwardly, Cat asked them to leave and called up her friend Claire.

Claire was mother hen of their friendship group. Not that she was over caring and sensitive, but more that she was bossy, nosy and extremely opinionated. Cat wanted her with her more than any of the other women as she would know what to say, she would make the tea and fuss about the house. She would deal with any phone calls and hopefully she would have a bottle of vodka with her too. Claire would know what to do, know what to say and not ask the wrong sort of questions.

7.

When Claire received the call from Cat early Saturday afternoon, she was in the middle of giving her husband Wayne a back massage. And when they heard the phone ringing, Wayne told her not to answer it. He was enjoying the moment to the point of either falling asleep or getting a hard –on. He was determining in his mind where this massage was heading, aware that their two boys were still in their own bedrooms, probably playing on the Xboxes and probably still in their pyjamas on a lazy Saturday, and they could easily stay distracted for hours to come. Claire however, wasn't in the mood for afternoon delight as Wayne liked to call it. She was too hungover and tired from the night before as she'd polished off a suitable amount of wine at home with Wayne and they'd binged on a takeaway Chinese. She was still feeling full, feeling heavy and her head was pounding, and so she climbed off Wayne's back, leaving him lying on the sofa and went to answer her phone.

Within minutes she had told Cat she was on her way round. She quickly threw on some more appropriate clothing and gave enough instructions to make sure Wayne took the boys with him if he was planning on going out anyway. The pair of them were in utter shock.

Wayne was a kids Rugby coach too and spent a lot of his spare time with Billy and the other guys at the Rugby club. He also had a lot of time for Cat. He liked her svelte, quasi glamorous look, compared to the homely rounder figure of his own wife. When they were out with friends he was always impressed with the effort that Cat made, and the subtle sexiness to her often understated attire. He would never admit it but he had a bit of a thing for her, from a distance only though. He secretly liked watching her jog past his lounge window as she so often did, in her tight lycra vest and shorts, leaving extremely little to the imagination. He often found himself waiting by the window, when he thought she might be out for a run, and would instigate conversations with her when they were out to try and pin a time down. She was his fantasy, something he had never told anyone else, not even as a joke. By the time she reached his house on her jog, glistening beads of sweat had started to form around her neck and hairline, and more specifically, under her bust. Her pert nipples poignant through her tight vest, the shape of her bum in her colourful leggings and the concentration and innocence in her face. Yes, he really did fancy Cat and many of his private moments had her picture in his mind, but he hoped he was very careful not to let on when they were out together. He loved his wife Claire very much, they had been together for over 20 years and had a fantastic marriage. Claire was very loving, very obliging and had a great set of boobs. She had a real woman's figure that no man in his right mind would turn away from, and she certainly knew how to use her body too. But Claire was starting to show her age. She was putting on weight, becoming less frisky, so he would have to ask for it more than she offered now and she was generally trying less. He'd bought her gym membership for her birthday in the hope that she would take the hint, but all she did was Aqua Aerobics once a week, and she wasn't going to burn off the pounds prancing around the pool like an idiot. He realised after he had bought it that she thought the membership was easy access to Lattes and Cappuccinos in the new café at the club. Claire was also his best friend though, and he wasn't going to cheat on her with her sexy friend, who had now shockingly become a widow. The words just didn't sound right, you didn't become a widow in your 40s. The group couldn't just lose one of their gang overnight. It just couldn't be true!

Claire arrived at an open door and made her way straight into the kitchen, where Cat was unmoved from the sofa. The women hugged each other and Claire immediately went to put the kettle on and put the used cups that Richard and Lee had left on the side in the dishwasher. "What the fuck is wrong with men?" she muttered under her breath as she cleared up their mess. Realising the error of her words, she shut up and made her way back over to Cat. It took a while for Cat to really acknowledge her friend there and even longer before she was ready to talk. But Claire was fine with that, she knew her role and her role was a mix of doing, listening and just being.

When she finally started to speak, Cat's sentences were short and didn't make a great deal of sense. Question after question of Why and How and What the. There were no answers to be given just yet and Claire patiently sat cuddled up to her friend nodding and attending. Two cups of tea later, Cat changed her questions to statements. She suddenly turned to Claire and blurted out "He had been a complete dickhead this week. An absolute bastard. And now he's dead!"

"I don't know if you should be talking like that", Claire answered her quietly. It was very unlike Cat to bad mouth anyone in front of other's, especially her own husband whom she defended continuously to anyone who might have a negative word to say about him. And he was dead. Why would you speak ill of the dead so soon after finding out? "But he was!" Cat argued. "He's been a bully, he's spiteful and had absolutely no interest in me at all, even with the boys away this week. I can't believe he's gone though, I'm waiting for him to come through the door any moment now and demand some food. Maybe I should get the bacon out of the freezer" her words floated off as she realised herself that she wasn't making any sense.

Claire, for the first time in as long as she could remember, was stunning into silence. What do you say to a grieving widow who is now seriously slagging off her dead husband? What she really wanted to do was join in the slagging match, get all the dirt from Cat and find out exactly what her husband had been up to behind closed doors, in the privacy of their home. She loved nothing more than other people's gossip, but she still had a little tact left in her. Her problem was easily and quickly solved by Cat offering more information without prompting. "Do you want to know what he was really like?" she asked. Well, Claire thought. She did ask, and it's only right of me to let her speak.

And so Cat told Claire about Billy. How he would bully her verbally, call her nasty names just to get a reaction and give him some enjoyment. He had thrown her home cooked food into the bin, or worse, onto the floor when he didn't like the look of it. How he would take the piss out of her in front of the children and make them mock her alongside him. How he never told her what time he would be coming home and how sex was mostly when he was blind drunk, very one-sided and far too forceful for her liking. "But do you know what has really pissed me off most?" Cat asked Claire rhetorically. "I put up with that because I can, and I'm either a complete muppet or a dickhead, but I think he was shagging Natalya. I've got a horrible feeling, and probably proof if I think about it, that they were having an affair behind my back!"

Claire was lapping up all this information, this was pure gossip gold and something she would have to think very wisely about before reusing, but hearing Cat say that she thought her husband had been screwing their friend was something else. She thought back to the time they were at Jaycee and Simon's. How Claire, Cat and Jaycee had secretly commented on the lack of material in Natalya's dress, how she really did look like mutton dressed as lamb and really didn't realise it. How Claire and Jaycee noticed Natalya walking out of the kitchen and returning quite some time later looking much more dishevelled than when she had left. Had they known then? Realised what was happening but put it to the back of their minds? Had they brushed it off as they were a close group of friends who supposedly trusted each other and clearly wouldn't screw one another over? Claire had to find out the truth now to satiate her appetite. But Natalya wouldn't tell her, especially now that she had no reason to, if it were indeed true. 50% of her secret was lying dead in a morgue. Claire would have to speak to Jaycee and the two of them could decide what they wanted to believe. Would she tell Wayne too? What would he think? She knew that Wayne had a roaming eye, he tried not to let on, but Claire was too aware of her own surroundings to miss the glances that Wayne gave her friends. She wasn't stupid, but she was more confident than most that he wouldn't do anything. They had a strong marriage. He had never thrown away the food she cooked, and was never rude to her in front of their boys. She would always satisfy him when he wanted sex or something else. She had made sure that he had very little time for an affair.

The problem is when a tight group of friends are together for so many years, people change, things happen that aren't always to be shared as they might have once been. The secrets in their group were slowly unravelling, but Claire herself wasn't ready to reveal her own. She knew Wayne was looking at her friends, so quite equally, she would often look at his friends too. She knew how much of a flirt Billy was and the way he was around Natalya, and she thought some of that attention was due for herself too.

Claire thought back to the time, about six months previously, quite a while before Billy had shagged Natalya at their friends' house, but was still showing a total lack of respect for his own wife with his comments and looks towards other women. Claire herself had decided to get in on the action with Billy and his roaming hands. She had made a move on Billy.

Another party, another house. The families got together so often, it was easy to lose track of what happened at whose house, and whether the kids were there or not. Often the kids would be dragged along to their party nights, and would lock themselves away with a few consoles and a large screen. They rarely came out to see the adults unless they were hungry or needed the loo. Occasionally the younger ones would just fall asleep wherever they were playing and by the time the parents decided to call it a night, they would get swept up into a father's arms, or gently woken up for the walk home.

Anyway, there had been an occasion, when Claire, drunk again, had had a row with Wayne just before they were heading out. They had rowed about money. Wayne wasn't making the commission he was used to making at work, Conservatories were not as popular as they had been ten years previously and as a result the money coming in at home was cut by a considerable amount. Claire however, hadn't cut back on her spending, despite Wayne asking her on more than a few occasions. Was there really a need for a new pair of shoes, three new handbags and indoor skiing lessons in June? Claire loved to spend money as often as she could. She loved to show off to anyone who might be paying her a bit of attention, and as she didn't work, she had that opportunity every day. She just loved to look around the shops, to accessorise her look to make herself more trendy and appealing, trying to get that sexier look and hopefully less frumpy. She would buy diet pills online and treatments to make herself look slimmer without having to do the exercise or cut out the drinking. Some of these treatments ran into the thousands when she was advised that a session of 6 treatments would give the best results. Wayne couldn't see any difference in her appearance and had flipped when she pulled the label off a new pair of shoes to wear on that particular evening. Claire went into a strop, she was used to shopping and used to being a lady of luxury. She was not going to change a habit that brought her so much happiness. She had earned this right. By the time they arrived at the party, they'd stopped talking to one another and went off in opposite directions. Wayne was quite happy to leave her to it and forget about her whilst he was with his friends. Claire didn't tell her friends that they were rowing, as despite her love of other people's gossip, she hated to be subject of anyone else's. This was a private matter, between her and Wayne but when Billy came into the kitchen to pour a fresh drink at the same time as her, and they were the only two there, she thought she might try and have a little fun.

She was a good flirt, always knew how to turn heads with her ample cleavage, shoulders back, leaning in to whisper rather than shout across the room. She had said something to Billy and he had laughed, he was always up for a bit of flirting and it was obvious that he loved the attention from any woman. She had then brushed his arm with her bust as she reached over to get the prosecco bottle. "Are you in a naughty mood?" she had whispered so gently into his ear. He immediately grabbed her wrist and pulled her hand down to his hardening crotch. No words were needed as she performed a quick but professional hand job on his excited shaft. Billy shuddered with delight "I would prefer your lips around my cock!" Billy had whispered back to Claire "but now is not the time". Claire pushed herself closer to Billy, expecting him to reciprocate the favour and touch her back, "we have a little more time" she whispered, but he kept one hand firmly around his beer glass and the other flat on the table top. He decided when he had had enough and pushed her away so he could go to the bathroom to finish himself off and clean up. He didn't speak to Claire again that evening. She was hurt. He didn't even glance over at her with a knowing recognition. She had done something she would never normally have considered, but she had needed the attention. She hadn't got what she wanted and now felt used and extremely stupid.

On another occasion some weeks later, the group of friends had all been chatting about everything and nothing, when Claire had mentioned about picking up something that had dropped on the floor and Billy had replied that she had a fantastic grip. Hardly anyone in the conversation picked up on what he said but Claire knew exactly what he was referring to. How dare he talk about her like that in front of their friends, and how dare he not have tried to please her as she had him. Her lust had turned to anger and bitterness.

Claire stayed with Cat for the rest of the day. The tea became wine and the two women sat together talking, not talking, crying, not crying. Before Claire went home, she and Cat had planned who else needed to be contacted, who should be at home with her when the boys came home tomorrow from their grandparents and how they were going to sort out the funeral. Of course there had to be a post-mortem first but they could start contacting funeral parlours and booking a room for the wake. Billy would want a big send off, and a lot of booze. That was something that no one would argue with.

8.

Carly had her victim. He has been confirmed and verified and the boxes were all ticked. But now she had to find his murderer, the motive and possibly a weapon. This was more than she ever imagined she would be investigating in sleepy little Oldcoewood but she was never one to turn down a challenge and an opportunity. She was very grateful for the support she had around her, and fully aware that she was definitely not the lead on this case, but she was going to do everything in her power to make sure she caught the perpetrator as smartly and quickly as she possibly could.

Having been home for a few hours to rest and try and recoup, she took a stroll down to the small but well stocked shop in the town and bought post-it notes and a few sheets of the largest white paper she could get hold of. She was going to recreate the office wall in her spare room, so that she could add and analyse the case whenever she thought of something new to add. She could then take that information and add it to the official board back at the station.

She knew from her training with the force and her extensive research into everything police and detective related, that where previously the statement that most victims knew their killer stood ground, this had now changed. Actually only 1% of males killed in 2018 were killed by their partners and one in 4 men were killed by a friend or associate but over a third of murders were conducted by a stranger. Scrap these facts, Carly thought. They aren't going to help the case at all. Oldcoewood wasn't a big town, neighbourhood watch was rife, whether authorised patrols or twitching behind the curtains. She needed to know and investigate everyone who knew Billy. This was going to take some time, but it was crucial that she didn't miss anyone out.

As an obvious starter, she printed out photos from Billy's facebook page of his friends and family. A lovely picture of Cat, must have been taken at a wedding or something as she had a very typically floral guest dress on and a fascinator in her beautiful blonde hair. Carly thought back to her meetings with Cat, it was so difficult to tell at this stage, she was obviously a grieving wife. But Carly had noticed when she was in their house, there weren't lots of photos of the couple up on the walls, mostly just of the children and one obligatory wedding photo. The two couches in the lounge both looked equally worn. That could be because of numerous visitors to the house, but it also could be because Billy and Cat liked to sit separately when relaxing in the evening. That could mean absolutely nothing but she was profiling their relationship and calling on every memory she had of being in their house and writing it down. She recalled Cat putting on make-up before going to identify her husband. Was that out of habit, that he didn't like to see her without it or shock, as shock did extremely strange things to people, and there was no doubt that Cat was in shock when Carly and James had broken the news to her.

She liked Cat, she thought as she pinned her photo to the wall and wrote a post-it note above with her details on. "Nothing immediately obvious there, but one to return to in a short while. Let's move on to the next suspect" she muttered out loud to her French Bulldog, Frenchie who had just walked into the room to see what was going on.

The next two suspects were Lee and Richard, who had been out with Billy on Friday night. Their photos went up on the wall, along with their wives. Carly stopped short of adding their children. She really couldn't see how a twelve year old child would murder someone, although she wasn't so naïve that she knew it didn't happen, just maybe not in Oldcoewood! She would put the children to one side for an absolute emergency if every single other trail ran cold. She had a gut feeling though that she wouldn't be bringing any children into the station for interviews.

An hour later and half of the wall was already full of photos of Billy's friends and family, other members of the Rugby club, bar owners and of course young Pete, who had found the body in the first place. Although she hoped she would rule Pete out first because he was a really nice guy, worked hard for the community and seriously did look petrified when he first showed them the body in the river. She also knew that he had been high as a kite when he'd bumped into them as he ran out of the field, in no fit state at all to conduct a clever murder, hiding evidence and ensuring the body was dragged far enough away from the road to be found where it was.

Carly took a break from her picture wall to call in for any news from forensics. She was in luck as they had just been sent over to the unit. She decided to go to the station to add her notes to the wall there and see for herself.

Billy had indeed been strangled but he had also experienced some trauma from a hit on the back of the head with a blunt instrument. So no knives, no guns but residue from a rock, of which there must be a few thousand down at the river, many of them submersed under the water, so a very, very slim chance of fingerprints from the implement that might have been used to bash Billy around the head. The strangler had worn gloves or something over their hands, as there were no prints on Billy's neck either, but there was bruising, finger shaped bruising around his throat. This was definitely a contributing factor to his demise. It was difficult to determine the size of the fingers by the neck bruises, they were quite constant around the whole of the neck area, so no clue as to whether small or large hands had done the deed.   And of course there was also the question of Billy's attire, or lack of it. He was found only in his boxer shorts. Who had removed his clothes and why would they? Had he removed his own clothes before meeting his assailant? It wasn't a robbery, as his wallet had been found and there was still some money and his cards in it. It did seem like extra effort on behalf of the perp. who would already have made the decision on where and how to murder Billy, as it was evident that this murder was planned. Was he taken to the river after he died? There were no drag marks along the bank or the grass verge. Was he dragged down the river itself and then planted up by the bridge, hauled out of the water rather than drawn into it? Was he taken to the river whilst he was alive? Billy wasn't a small man and chances are there would have been a hell of a struggle if he hadn't willingly taken part in the midnight river walk.

Carly was extremely thorough, writing all her questions down in her notebook, prepared to spend quite a few hours assembling the answers with her interviews and further research. She would have to cancel lunch with her brother and his new wife on Sunday because when she was in the zone, she was absolutely not prepared to zone out in order for roast chicken and all the trimmings, tempting as it might be! But they would understand, they had been more than supportive when Carly joined the force and promised to support her along her journey of making the world a better, safer place, one step at a time!

The adrenaline was flowing, and her blank pages were quickly filling. She had the photos up, and she needed to get around to interviewing everyone in those photos. Richard and Lee were the last friends known to have seen Billy before his death, and so they would be first on her list of official interviews.   She called PC Gold and DI Sidhu and told them of her plan. It was a great plan, and so in depth. Sidhu was pleased that she was being so proactive. He was earmarking her for future promotions and her enthusiasm for the job would be a great plus point on her files.

 Daniel Gold loved working with Carly. He was also ambitious and enthusiastic but with his perfect wife and beautiful baby at home now, he had no wish to put himself back on the streets of London where the risk was so much higher. His wife, Sarah was extremely paranoid about his role in the police, having witnessed a police officer being attacked when she was at University in Liverpool. She had called the emergency services when it happened, and although the attack hadn't been fatal, it had certainly been life changing and the officer in question didn't return to his job on the force. She had lived with the memories and often had nightmares about them even now, over 6 years later. When she met Daniel, he was already on the London streets of Tower Hamlets and it caused a lot of friction in their relationship. He had dreamed of nothing more than joining the police force when he was younger, and when the opportunity arose to work in one of the busiest parts of London for the police force, he had jumped at it, not taking into account the dangers surrounding him. when his relationship with Sarah became more serious and they talked about marriage and settling down, that's when they came to a compromise that he could still follow his dream and remain in the force, but he would also choose his beat carefully and locate to a nicer part of the country where they could live and work with less risk to his life and her mental health. Sarah could then become a part of the community in which he worked, keeping a close eye on him. They were both happy with the decision to move to Oldcoewood and Sarah had gotten herself a job working for the council, processing planning applications and building relationships with all the other council workers and police force. It gave her comfort that she knew those who were working alongside her husband and a false sense of security that she felt if she knew what was going on locally, then she could manage her preconceived ideas about it.

Sarah also liked PC Carly Cook. Following her initial distrust of such a good looking female officer working so closely with her husband, Carly had managed to alleviate her fears and make her realise that the relationship was built on a close working connection, and the friendship that formed from this bond would include her too. She had gone from having a knotted stomach on hearing about PC Carly Cook to excitement on hearing of what her husband's colleague had been up to.

This made life so much easier for Daniel. He couldn't have wished for a better work partner, and understanding that his wife was of a nervous disposition, he was proud of Carly and the work she had put in to make Sarah feel at ease. It meant he could get on with doing the best job with the best partner and could go home at the end of the day and talk to his wife about Carly, knowing that she wouldn't get jealous. But right now, he was telling Sarah that his Saturday was now going to be spent interviewing a number of people in connection with Billy's death, instead of spending time at home with his family. Of course Sarah knew who Billy was. She had friends in her baby groups with older siblings who played rugby. Billy was well known in a number of different circles. She decided she would go round to her mother's for the day and be pampered whilst the baby was looked after by a doting grandmother and her husband was hard at work.

Daniel and Carly arranged to meet, made a few necessary phone calls and requested Richard to come into the station for their first interview as soon as possible.

9.

Richard didn't want to leave his wife on that Saturday afternoon. She was still lying on the couch, acting as if she were on her deathbed. She had been demanding tea and water intermittently obviously craving attention much more than the actual drinks, and Richard, still in shock from the news of his friend, had obligingly followed her orders. He was happy to be distracted by his beautiful Diva, but in his mind he knew he needed to go in to the police station and clear his name. He had never been suspected or accused of anything major before. Of course he'd received speeding fines and parking fines and once at university he'd been cautioned for a small amount of weed in his possession, but he was generally a good law abiding citizen. He certainly hadn't ever been called on as a suspect in a murder case, the thought terrified him and the beads of sweat had already started to form on his brown. He desperately wanted to help too, anything he could offer that would assist in finding the bastards that had taken his friend from him. Knowing he was one of the last people to see him alive was a frightening prospect too and he felt a responsibility to try and paint as clear a picture as he could for the police.

He told Natalya he would be back as soon as he could, and warned the children to behave and be good to their mother. The children decided they would stay in their own rooms and leave her alone for some peace and quiet. It was safer that way for everyone. There was nothing for them to gain from spending time with their mother when she had been in for another one of her cosmetic ops.

Richard arrived at the station and was taken through to an interview room by PC Gold. Carly was already waiting for him there. The two police officers were polite and friendly to him, which put him the slightest bit at ease. The questioning was straightforward. He had to really remember the whole evening, but because he had had about 8 pints and a few chasers, his memory wasn't as clear as it could have been.

Nevertheless he racked his brain to recall as much as he could and talk through the evening, how he had turned up to the Dog and Duck pub in the centre of town, and Billy and Lee were already propping up one of the tall tables with a couple of empty glasses alongside their half full ones. There weren't any bar stools at the table as they had all been taken to increase capacity at other tables, so he remembered they stood for the evening. He recalled how they chatted together, they did eye up some of the younger ladies as they sashayed passed, brushing body parts either due to the pub being pretty full, or purely because they were flirting and loving the attention, on their way to the toilets or the smoking area outside, they clearly enjoyed the looks they were receiving, Richard was sure he hadn't acted inappropriately towards any of them. He recalled at one point seeing Cat with her friends and had stopped very briefly to say hello before going to the loo himself. The men had chatted rugby, football, women and even thrown in the weather, but then Richard's memory began to falter. They drank a lot, they laughed a lot but at the end of the night, Lee ran out of the pub to be sick and Richard had followed a few minutes after to check he was ok. When he looked back, Billy had disappeared. "I walked off with Lee, after he had thrown his guts up in a bush." said Richard, "We didn't see Billy again, so assumed he'd thought we'd gone home already and pissed off himself. We don't exactly check on each other getting home safely like the girls do. It's a bit poofy to do that really, isn't it?" He hung his head, reflecting how the girls always say to one another "Text me when you're home" and how they always did. Men just didn't do that, they expected each other to just arrive home and the next contact they would have with one another was to arrange the next night out or send a message about a game.

Richard was visibly shaken, and Carly could see that he was genuinely shocked. She closely monitored his eye movement, his hands and his general body language. If he was lying then he was a fantastic actor. She asked a few more questions, made sure she had everything that she wanted at this stage, wrapped up the interview and thanked Richard for his time. As Richard left, he passed his friend Lee on his way in. They hugged each other, Lee looking equally as shocked and upset as his friend was. Neither men had the look of a killer about them, but then having said that Carly had never actually met a killer face to face before, and her training was to know better than surmise a specific look! Still, her gut instinct told her that these two were innocent, their alibi was the amount they had to drink and their inability to function properly as a result. The stale smell of alcohol still seeping through the overlaid aftershave. And Richard's timing that he gave for his journey home was spot on from leaving the pub to arriving home, his Ring doorbell confirmed this.

The interview with Lee was extremely similar to the one with Richard. Again Carly paid close attention to his body language, the way his eyes moved when he was thinking of the answers he was giving. The look of sorrow as he spoke about his late friend. She really couldn't see how either of these two friend's would have the power and force in their drunken states to take their mate, their drinking buddy, down to the river and strangle him. Why would they have stripped him down to his underwear either? What would the motive and the reasoning be. A stupid drinking game gone wrong? But both men returned home fully clothed themselves and certainly not wet or muddy from being by the river.

Carly and Dan compared their notes and both had come to a similar conclusion. Carly wouldn't strike them off her list completely but she would move them to the bottom of it. "On to the next ones", she turned to Dan and sighed. He nodded in agreement and went off to top up their coffee cups.

CCTV reviews came back too, to show that both Lee and Richard were seen walking along one of the main roads towards their houses around the times they both confirmed. They wouldn't have had time to take and dump the body after leaving the pub and get back home as was shown on the cameras. The two officers reported their findings to their DI, explaining how unlikely it could be for either Richard, Lee or even both together to have murdered Billy. "You two are doing good, keep it up" he said to them when they told him. "I've told the wider team that any insight they have they are to pass it on to you two to decipher and manage". He recognised that it was a huge jump in responsibility for both of them, but could see how much effort they were putting into the case, and was confident that he had the right team in place. James Sidhu had no qualms about explaining his decisions to his seniors and believed they would agree with the choices he had made thus far.

CCTV was proving to be worth its weight in gold. Further footage that came back showed Billy walking alone just a couple of minutes after his friends. However, he didn't follow the straight route that they took and was seen to be turning off down the narrow side street by the Dog and Duck which meant that after a couple of minutes he was out of sight of the cameras. Additional searches underway would bring up if and where he was picked up again by the cameras further on his journey. The CCTV was a major assist in putting a timeline on the movements of Friday night. Carly was in regular contact with those checking every detail from the cameras. She wanted them to know that she was grateful, and this was urgent. It was their jobs, but it didn't hurt to reiterate her gratitude and further cement her working relationships with those in the team. She hoped that she would be buying quite a few pints following this case when she could thank everyone more personally.

Another quick call from Carly to the team onsite by the river determined there was still no sign of the rest of Billy's clothing. Whoever had done this to him had left his wallet but taken his jeans and Tshirt. Strange but probably extremely significant, something she immediately wrote up on the wall. Excited but exhausted and running the risk of burning out already, Carly knew she had to stop at some point but the adrenaline was flowing too much. She hadn't been to bed since Thursday evening and desperately needed some time to recuperate her mental and physical strength to carry on with her investigation and interviews the next day. She decided that she had to call it a day there. It was Saturday afternoon and many of the analytics wouldn't get finalised until the beginning of the new week now anyway..

Carly said her goodbyes to the team at the station and headed off for home. She picked up a large kebab and chips on her way, large because she knew her greedy dog would want to share it with her and thought about what she could watch on Netflix. Whilst sharing her meal with Frenchie, Carly planned her agenda for the following day: the missing clothing was high on that agenda, she would naturally need to speak to Cat again, probably in person, rather than calling, and set up some more interviews with Billy's friends, other pub goers and the staff who had been on duty that Friday night. She would then look at Billy's work life, more about his personal life and complete the full picture of who Billy Ashton was.

10.

CAT

Sunday morning loomed, and Cat woke up feeling sick. The children were coming home today and she would have to break the news to them. She wouldn't allow her parents to do it, it was far too much of a burden to put them on, and so they had delayed saying anything to Ned and Jason. Naturally they were distraught, and having to hide it from the boys was beyond difficult. Cat had spoken to one of the Police family liaison officers who had advised her on how to tell them. It still didn't make it any easier, and having extra time to prepare made it worse. She was dreading the moment they would walk through the door, full of stories about their fun week away, excited to be home again and she would take all that joy away from them. A small vodka, but just a small one as it was only half past 10 in the morning, managed to take the edge of the pure fear rushing throughout her body. She got herself washed and dressed, did her hair and make up as she had done every morning when Billy had been sitting in the other room, or lazing in bed when there was no Rugby practice. She also declined the offer from Claire to come round and sit with her whilst she told the boys, as kind as it was of Claire to offer. But her parents would be there soon enough, that would help her considerably.

Cat wasn't a stranger to the police, she had come across them more than her fair share of times in her past. This time she was grateful for the help they were giving her and impressed with the speed in which this young policewoman in particular was dealing with her husband's case. Both Lee and Richard had messaged her the evening before to say they had already been in to the station to give a statement. Her own relationship with the police however, hadn't always been the best. There were things about Cat and her past life that she had shared with no one, not even her own husband. She had buried secrets that she consciously kept as deeply buried as she could.

Cat had studied languages at Birmingham University. Her parents had preferred that she stayed locally in Nottingham so they could support her financially and also emotionally, but Birmingham offered her the best course, and it wasn't like she was going anywhere as far away as Aberdeen or Plymouth.

Judy and Tony Montague, Cat's parents, had witnessed and lived with a teenage Cat being influenced by the wrong crowds at school. They weren't ignorant. They knew their daughter was pretty and intelligent, and had used this on many occasions to get her own way. When she was at high school, she had picked out the group of girls she wanted to be associated with and had wormed her way into their gang, often pushing others out if they deemed to be a threat to her. She had no end of male admirers and her parents were sure she was a lot younger than they would have wished for when she had her first sexual encounter. In fact, what they didn't know for quite a long time was that she had been just 14 years old, and he was 19. Cat had met him when she was out with her friends after school one day. They were just hanging around the streets of Nottingham, bored, restless and fed up with the homework that was due in the following day. Ironically another William, but known as Will to his friends, the girls had spotted him and his mates and made the right noises to get their attention. Will and his friends were also bored and looking to cause a bit of trouble. A few introductions and a great deal of flirting led to Cat and Will leaving the group after a short space of time. He had led her down an alleyway, behind Domino's pizza where she had given her first blow job. That led to the start of a semi- secret relationship, in which Will would text to arrange to meet her, usually out in public and then they would go off and find somewhere as hidden as possible to have sex. Cat was excited by the prospect of having an older boyfriend. It made her so much more mature than her peers, and the snippets of information she gave them, some of it true, some of it embellished, put her high up on the pedestal of her group. When they were out they were reckless and got told off on a number of occasions for loitering, underage drinking and disturbing the peace. Cat always managed to avoid her parents finding out. She was still their blue eyed baby who could do no wrong, and she was confident that she was playing them right into her hands, the way she wanted it to be. That meant that she certainly couldn't have ever asked her mother to help her get the pill. On most occasions Will was careful and used a condom, but a few times, when emotions were high, he reassured her that they would be fine. And of course Cat fell pregnant. She had just turned 15, it was about three weeks after her birthday and Will had bought her a litre bottle of vodka. They had drunk it with just a couple of his friends around, lying in a hidden part of the park where they knew they were out of sight. Will had told her he would be careful and assured her that you couldn't fall pregnant if you were drunk anyway. They had sex in the park, but his friends were watching, and although Cat didn't like the idea of an audience, she was too drunk to protest. It had been quick and messy and Will's friends had laughed at the fumbling going on before they got bored and roamed off.

A month later, Cat was ill. She had never felt this ill in her life, and her mother was really concerned. But Cat refused to go to the doctor. She told her Mum it was just stomach flu and she was happy to stay in bed and sleep it off. Cat needed her mum to be out of the house, so that she could call Will and tell him, because she had read enough books, and watched enough teen movies to know that it wasn't flu, but she was pregnant. When she finally managed to get rid of her mum by asking her to buy her a magazine and some sweets, she called Will and whispered down the phone to him. Will hadn't taken the news well at all. "You have to get rid of it" he said immediately. "I'll get arrested if you tell anyone you had sex with me," he continued angrily. "So you have a choice. Get rid or I deny even knowing you."

Cat was petrified, she didn't know what to do. She begged Will to help her as she knew she couldn't ask anyone else. it would ruin her reputation and destroy the relationship she had with her parents. Eventually he said he would find somewhere for her to go for an abortion. He went as far as taking her to the clinic and then left her at the door. His final remarks to her were "this is way too scary; I can't be dealing with this. You're better off finding someone your own age". He walked off, leaving her in tears outside the door of the clinic. She had been dumped. Frightened, without help from anyone else and very sick. Thankfully, a woman from the clinic had witnessed the scene out of her window and went to bring Cat in. Naturally Cat had lied about her age convincingly and went through with the abortion, completely on her own and petrified.

After that incident Cat became withdrawn. She took a couple of weeks off school to recover, still refusing the help from her worried mother, and when she returned, she refused to spend time with her group of friends. They tried for a little while to get her to talk to them. They wanted to know if there was another reason behind her illness, but she wasn't going to tell anyone. They soon gave up asking. Cat had become boring and they didn't have time for boring. It meant though that she took more care with her studies, and her school work improved. Her parents knew that something had happened to bring on this change, but didn't know the full extent. They were timid people themselves and didn't want to pry into her life any more at the risk of scaring her away, and so they left her to her own devices, whilst making sure they were around for her should she call out of them.

As a result of everything that had happened to her, Cat did well in her exams and secured a place easily at Birmingham University. She had lengthy discussions with her parents about moving to Birmingham, they tried their hardest to keep her at home with them, ignoring the fact that she had her future ahead of her. They just didn't want to cut the apron strings and let their daughter out into the wild. Judy knew she wasn't mentally ready for this, but she couldn't persuade her daughter any other way. Cat was adamant that she was going to move away. The course in Birmingham was very detailed, very encompassing, and included a year away in one of the countries whose languages she was studying. Whether that would be France or Spain she hadn't decided but she was pleased to be leaving Nottingham and making a new start. She didn't want to keep in touch with any of her school friends, she was constantly scarred with the memories of Will and the pain and shame of the abortion that burnt deep within her.

With a fresh start, the old confident and flirty Cat gradually came out of hiding. Tired of being alone and studious, Cat was ready to be popular again. As she had when she had started high school, she found it easy to pick her ideal group of friends and be the person she wanted to be. She didn't talk about her home life. This was her new life, and had nothing to do with her past. She loved the attention she was getting again; she loved flirting and definitely wasn't put off having relationships. This time she could go to the doctor and get herself put on the pill. Older and wiser, the past was firmly behind her.

For her first University year at least. And then things changed.

She was in the first term of her second year at Uni. She had moved out of halls into a shared house with some girlfriends, and was enjoying the independence even more. She and her friends had a great social life, guys wanted to be with them, girls wanted to be like them and if they weren't out partying in the clubs and bars of Birmingham then they would often have a party at home, much to the annoyance of their neighbours. They had a name for themselves, they were definitely the most popular girls around campus and they all loved it. But then Will turned up at one of their house parties.

When Cat first saw him, it took a moment for her to recognise him. He had grown a beard and put on a bit of weight, but it was the glint in his bright blue eyes that she identified, and all her memories from her high school years back home came flooding back. Will had been invited by her housemate, who had met him in a local bar. He now lived in Birmingham, and worked as an Estate Agent. Cat's friend Emily was quite taken by him, and excited to introduce this new guy to her friends. "How nice to meet you!" Will greeted Cat as if he'd never set eyes on her before. Cat did a double take, then ran out of the room, up to the shared bathroom and threw up. How dare he come into her home and look at her as if she didn't matter. After all that she had been through because of him.

Emily ran upstairs to look for Cat, and when she found her in the bathroom, she assumed that she'd had a little too much to drink. Speechless, Cat didn't try and correct her but let her friend stroke her hair and tell her that now she had thrown it all up, she could start drinking again. Emily happily skipped back downstairs to her new man. Cat followed down a while later to find Emily and Will in a compromising embrace splayed over the threadbare couch in the lounge.

Emily and Will continued to see each other. Emily was smitten and Cat didn't know what to do about it. Will mostly stayed out of her way, until one afternoon, when Emily was still at Uni, and Cat came home to find Will lying on the sofa watching telly. She finally found her voice to confront him. "You've got a fucking liberty," she started. "Coming into my life again and treating me as if you don't even know me!"

Will smiled at her. "Wanna continue where we left off?" he slyly suggested. "You're old enough now and still fucking sexy. You can't deny it, we had a good time back then didn't we?"

Cat was visibly sickened. She couldn't have this man in her home any longer. He was stopping her from getting on with her life, from being the new person she had worked hard to become. But she was still not prepared to share her story with anyone. Emily wouldn't believe her if she tried to tell her who Will really was. Emily and Cat, despite being good friends, didn't have a close trusting relationship. Cat had been caught kissing a previous boyfriend of Emily's and had to do a lot of grovelling and putting blame on this other guy taking advantage of her when she was drunk, to win back her trust, and finally Emily gave in and dumped the guy, citing girl love being stronger than a stupid, dickhead Uni student with his brain in his pants.

Cat had been relieved. She liked Emily, and they were all part of a good group of popular girls. She hadn't meant to kiss her boyfriend but the opportunity had arisen at a time when Cat was between lovers and needed the attention. She had been on her own with the guy, whilst Emily had run to the shops to buy more drinks. The chance was too strong not to turn down as she realised that she could wind him round her little finger.

She turned to Will "Get out my house now" she demanded. He smiled at her and made himself more comfortable on the sofa. "Get out!" She screamed at him.

"I'm waiting for my girlfriend to come home and give me the best damn blowjob of my life" he calmly answered. "You don't want me to tell her that you tried it on with me, like you did with her last boyfriend do you?"

Cat stormed up to her room, fuming. She had to get rid of this guy as soon as possible.

For days she hid herself away, thinking of how she could ensure her secret was kept safe, and finally, after over a week of stressing, pulling her hair out and close to running away, Will figuratively shot himself in the foot.

They all smoked weed at the house, it was normal, it was a student house after all, but Cat had never wanted to do anything stronger. Will and Emily however, liked to pop a few pills when they were out clubbing. It was the late 90's after all and no one batted an eyelid when it happened. Pills were regular weekend accessories. Will would always get the pills for the girls and their friends. No one asked where he got them from, but he would be the middleman and hand out their 'sweets' as they were leaving the house for the parties. Cat had a plan. It was quite dangerous and she hoped that Emily would be ok, but her plan was for Emily to overdose on pills, not to the extent that anything serious would happen to her, but so that she would need a little medical attention to pump the drugs out of her system and have questions asked about where she got them from.

That weekend was a big party weekend. Everyone was getting ready at their house, and she knew that Will kept his pills in the pocket of his jeans, that only came off when he was sleeping or shagging. She had to get a pill into Emily before Will gave her one. Emily was little, thin as a rake so the effect of two pills over one would be pretty obvious. The couple were in Emily's bedroom for most of the afternoon, door locked, and no prizes for guessing what was going on behind it. Eventually, Will emerged to go and have a shower. Cat went into Emily's room with two vodka and Cokes. "Thought we could have a cheeky drink while we're getting ready" she suggested.

"Good idea" Emily replied, barely paying any attention to Cat who was furiously looking around the room for Will's jeans. She spotted them lying on the floor by Emily's hair straighteners. "Oh can I borrow your straighteners too?" Cat asked. "Mine are on the blink I think"

"Sure" Emily answered, still not paying attention. She was too busy picking out the smallest outfit she had in her wardrobe. Cat slid her hand into the pocket of the jeans and found the little bag she was hoping to be in there. She subtly felt the opening of the bag, counted more than the required amount of pills and took one out. She then turned to the two drinks on the side and popped the pill into one of them. She watched as it fizzled a little.

"I know" she suggested further "Shall we neck these to get the blood really circulating?"

"Really?" Emily turned around to her. "Are you wanting to get really shitfaced tonight then?"

Cat smiled and thrust the drink into her friend's hand. "Ready… one… two …" They both threw back the drinks, down in one go. Emily shivered as she swallowed hers down.

"Cheers" Cat finished, and with the hair straighteners in hand, she left the room. An hour later, they were all ready to leave, Will fished into his pocket and took out his little bag. "Line up" he joked as he handed out the pills in exchange for some notes.

An hour into the party the effects of the overdose hit Emily. She started to feel overanxious, and began sweating uncontrollably. She put it down to the room being hot and carried on dancing, enjoying the moment with her friends and her sexy man. Cat hadn't taken her eyes off her. The anxiety started to give Emily palpitations and within minutes she was struggling to catch her breath, she felt like she was on fire and the last thing she remembered before passing out was a piercing pain that travelled right through her brain. Cat watched her friend fall down and waited a couple of seconds before screaming out. A crowd rushed to Emily and someone shouted out to call an ambulance. Cat pushed through the crowds, she had to be with her friend on the way to the hospital.

Emily was put onto a drip but she had fallen into a coma. This wasn't meant to have happened, and Cat was petrified. In her mind, Emily would have a scare and would be questioned about the pills she had taken, she could then lead the police to her supplier. But now she was lying in a hospital bed, unconscious and everyone was looking at Cat.

The police were called and came into the hospital room promptly. They asked a number of questions there before requesting that Cat escort them to the station. She needed them to know that she herself hadn't taken any drugs, that she wasn't a user and wasn't part of this. Her plan could still work, she just prayed that her friend would recover soon.

Within a couple of hours, Will was at the police station being questioned and Emily had started to stir from her coma. Cat felt a great sense of achievement. In the most awful way. Mixed with guilt and concern for her friend she had told the police that she always told Emily that drugs were a bad idea, but her boyfriend Will was more persuasive. They were going to interview him anyway, but she had given them a little more reason to probe further. Even if he didn't have any drugs in his possession at the party, he had a wallet full of notes and a very good reason to be detained.

Emily was released from hospital a few days later and was sent home to her family in Belfast. Cat went back to their house in Birmingham to look for clues in Emily's bedroom that would help the police arrest Will. There were plenty there, and she left it to the professionals to find. It didn't take long, and with his previous caution handling drugs the year before, Will was convicted and imprisoned for 7 years. That gave Cat time to finish her degree and get the hell out of Birmingham before he would be released.

She had to make sure that Will would never return into her life, she had to cut ties with all her Uni friends as well as her school friends. And when she moved to London she did just that. She focused on new beginnings for the 2nd time.

11.

Cat had spent a long time thinking about her past. She was praying that it wasn't going to catch up with her now. Since leaving University she had been squeaky clean, keeping her nose out of anything that might get her noticed. She was very quick to accept her new surname when she got married and had changed all her official documentation within weeks of receiving her marriage certificate. It had to stay that way. She had buried her past so deep that if it was found out now, she didn't think she would be able to cope with the consequences. Especially now that she was widow and a victim of her husbands murder.

But what if it did come back to haunt her? What if Will had found her and it was payback time. Cat was scared. She logged onto her social media accounts to check for any new friend requests or unknown activity on her accounts. She had never said anything further about the whole incident to Emily, who after coming out of hospital, did try to speak to Cat on a number of occasions. She had still been in touch with Will and they had written to one another a few times when he was in prison, during which he had always sworn that he hadn't done anything different to what they had normally done, that no one else had had a reaction like Emily had. Naturally one would put it down to a bad trip, but Emily wasn't new to the drug scene, she had been taking party drugs on and off for a few years.

Emily had tried to bring up the conversation with Cat, questioning her being in her room before they got ready to go out, something that Cat would have never normally done, as her dislike for Will, although Emily didn't know why, was very apparent. Cat had stood her ground, and sworn it was just about hair straighteners and drinking, and she had taken the opportunity to be with her friend when Will was out of the room. She had no one who could deny that and she had concreted her side of the story so solidly in her own mind that she almost believed her own innocence.

Will on the other hand, knew that he hadn't given Emily any more pills and although he hadn't been in contact with Cat since his arrest, she knew that he knew, and it meant that she could never really let her guard fully down, she would always have to be looking over her shoulder. She followed Will's path as best as she could, without having to contact anyone from her past, so she knew when he had been released from prison, but had no way of finding out where he was living or if he had moved out of Birmingham. But now that her husband was dead, she was panicking, what if he had found her and this was her punishment. There was no activity on her own accounts but she changed her passwords to be on the safe side.   She then logged into her fake account on facebook. It had no profile picture, no friends and no activity, but was a way to view people who may have blocked her other account. People from her past who weren't as private as she was. She typed in Will's name and his account popped up. There was no activity to be seen on his account either, despite it not being private, all she could see was a profile picture update from a few years ago.

Cat knew she should probably tell the Police about Will, but that would have to wait until times were really desperate. She was in no position to jeopardise her own life for something that had happened years ago. She hadn't wanted to know what happened to Emily though, as the thought of her being permanently damaged or scarred from her coma experience was something that she didn't need to feel any more guilt over.

The pacing seemed endless until finally, about half past 11, she heard a car pull up into the driveway. The boys were already fighting as they clambered out of the car, arguing over something to do with the Fortnight game. She could hear the noises but not the words. She opened the door and fell into her mother's arms. Despite their strained relationship, she knew she could rely on her mother for anything. The boys stopped their bickering immediately and looked at their mother, sensing something wasn't right. Cat's father ushered them all in the house and sat the boys down in the lounge. Cat was desperately trying to keep herself together as she sat down between them. "Something awful has happened," she started. "Daddy was involved in an accident, and now he's..." She didn't know how to make the words sound any lighter. She didn't want to use words that might confuse the boys. They had to realise straight away "He's dead." She said, clearly but bluntly. The boys both looked at her, numb with shock. Ned, the eldest one, wrapped his arms around his mother. Jason, who was only 8 years old, ran over to his grandmother and sank into her arms. He wept. "I want my dad," he cried. "I want to play Rugby with him".

"You can't" Ned answered, "Don't be stupid." Cat hated to reprimand Ned at this time, but Jason was in shock, they were all in shock. She gently whispered in his ear that his brother's emotions would show in a different way to his own. Grief was a very strange thing. Her family had never experienced it before. The boys hadn't ever lost anyone in their young lives before now. As the realisation slowly sunk in, and the first round of tears gradually subsided, Ned started to ask more questions. His eleven year old mind was thinking fast. Cat told him that his dad had drowned in the river. He didn't need to know that he'd been strangled, murdered. She would try and protect her children for as long as she could before the full truth came out.

But that angered Ned. He accused his father of doing stupid thing whilst being drunk. He always did stupid things when he was drunk. Like the time he and Wayne played cricket in the garden at 2am and the first hit smashed a massive hole in the glass of the patio doors. "Mum," he asked, "why did he go down to the river when he was drunk? Did he go swimming? It's too shallow for swimming. Why didn't he come home with the others?"

Of course Cat didn't have an answer for her son. She just held him closer to her and through deep breaths explained that the police were in the process of finding out why he had gone, who he had gone with and exactly what had happened.

The next few hours passed in a blur for the family. Jason really couldn't get to grips with the information he had been given, he fidgeted, knowing that he shouldn't leave the room, but at the same time wanted to fill the void with endless chit chat that was far too distracting for the others in the room , and so in the end Cat let him play on his Xbox whilst Ned, Cat and her parents sat almost motionless in the lounge, wondering what they could say to one another to avoid the lengthy silences, but really not wanting to say anything at all.

Eventually Cat's mother got up to make sandwiches and told the boys to unpack their bags and put their toys away. By the afternoon menial chat had resumed, the washing machine was on and Ned told his mother that he still wanted to go to school the following day. He was quite precise in putting his case across to her when she shook her head in immediate response. "I don't want to spend a day sitting still and quiet at home." he explained "I don't know how that would help you and not make you feel even sadder Mum! And there's nothing I can do here, is there?" he said. " I don't know what to do but at school I can do school stuff." He'd rather be with his friends, Cat understood that and the distraction might help him. And so she made the decision to send them both into school, and her parents were staying down anyway, so she wouldn't be alone. She would need to talk to the head teacher, and be on standby if she was needed. But her boys were strong. If they thought they could cope with questions from their friends at school whose parents would have told them what had happened, then they probably would be able to.

12.

Naturally word had travelled at extreme speeds through the small town of Oldcoewood and Cat had been checking her messages on Facebook. She didn't know Billy's password to be able to access his account but she could see hundreds of messages of sympathy coming through on his page. She would put some time aside when she was ready to read through them all, and decide then if she was in a position to reply. No one was expecting a reply, a few wanted dates for the funeral though. How could they be asking that on Facebook, when her husband was still lying in the morgue, being poked and prodded, investigated and scrutinised for any clues to his death? Her own Facebook page was full of messages from her friends, all offering their deepest sympathies and love. Offers of help with the children, help with cooking and looking after the house were also proposed. It was touching how people would rally around when there was a crisis. Cat didn't want any help in the house though, she had her mother fussing around her for the time being, and she was quite capable of cooking for her boys when she was alone. She'd never had any help before, and her emotions didn't affect the way she could boil some pasta or cook a chicken. As she thought this, she scolded herself. Why was she thinking so negatively? What did other wives do when their husbands had supposedly been murdered? 'Put it down to grief', she thought, trying to be nicer to herself 'and now I know how I cope. I'm not a wailer, a screamer, a questioner. I'm a mum who needs to be strong for her children and get through this shit.' She was almost content with her thoughts. She went back to scrolling through Facebook. Most of the mums from the boys' classes at school had sent her messages of condolences. Even the ones she didn't care for, and she knew the feelings were mutual. Everyone has a heart, or at least everyone wants everyone else to think that they do in public!

The headmistress of the school had obviously been made aware too, thanks to the police calling her to inform, and on Sunday afternoon, Cat received a call from her. They talked for a while about what everyone thought the best action for the children should be. The head teacher thought it might be too soon to have them back at school, and the boys might be in shock despite what Ned had told his mum, but Cat was determined to do what they wanted, and so eventually they came to the agreement that she would talk to the children, explain their options and they would choose, although she was quite suggestive that the boys would be coming in to school anyway. She agreed with the Head teacher that should they want to do something outside of the classroom activities, they would be allowed to take time for themselves. It was an awkward conversation, Cat wasn't happy that the head teacher's opinion differed from her own. Was she now going to have to justify her decisions despite not having a clue what she really was doing?

Cat flipped back over to Billy's Facebook page. There were a number of friends that she didn't recognise, some of them obviously worked for the same Insurance company, as the names weren't completely foreign to her, but there were a few she had absolutely no idea about. Whether they too were work colleagues or perhaps school and college friends or even old flames. Everyone was entitled to their own past and now wasn't the time to get jealous of other women befriending him. Then she saw a message about half way down the long train of messages that had been received from Saturday afternoon when news had apparently gotten out to the wider audiences. She must have missed it the last time she looked at them though. It was a name she didn't recognise at all and the profile picture didn't ring any bells either. In fact the photo was of a

Ferris Wheel, no identifiable faces on the wheel and it wasn't the one that had been in the Coes Green fair earlier in the year. The name of the sender was Finn Dunn. The message simply said "Play Fair!!!" What did that mean? Three exclamation marks after the two words. That wasn't a message of condolence, it seemed to be a warning. Was it strong enough to be a threat? Cat clicked on the name Finn Dunn. It was a private account. She couldn't see any information about this person, she couldn't see their friends or location. She went back to look at the message on Billy's page. Just two words. Potentially, this could just be some nasty troll showing the world that when most people want to show their kindness and sympathy, there are always those for whom Facebook is an opportunity for spite and menace, how trolls like to jump on the bandwagon of every situation. It could be nothing, but still she couldn't stop thinking about it.

Cat decided to call Carly Cook on her personal number and get her opinion on it.

Despite being early Sunday afternoon, Carly picked up the phone after just two rings. She recognised the number and was keen to show that her full support was with Cat. Carly listened as Cat told her about the Facebook message. Before she had finished speaking, Carly had Facebook up on her account and was logging a call with her IT department to try and give her full access to Billy's account and to investigate Finn Dunn. She couldn't see any more into Finn's account than Cat was able to. She looked at the "Play Fair!!!" message over and over. With those exclamation marks it was definitely a statement and not a well-wishing response.

The page was printed out, highlighted and ready to be put up in duplicate on the walls at home and at the station. Who hasn't been playing fair then with Billy, or vice versa? Could this be a link to his death? Did we have a note from the killer? Carly was overwhelmed with the excitement from the message. She told Cat that she would be in touch with her as soon as possible, and was taking this comment on Facebook extremely seriously.

Without any more evidence from the CCTV footage which would have to wait until Monday, Carly made a new list with all the names on her board and the heading of Play Fair. Play Fair could have something to do with rugby and she listed the Rugby dads under this heading. Could he really have been murdered over a game? It wasn't impossible and people had been killed over sports before, but this was kids Rugby. Would it be that competitive to end in murder? There must be other links to playing fair and it was her job to find them out. Cat had mentioned on her call that she was taking the children to school on Monday, maybe it would be a good chance to have an eavesdrop on the chat in the playground. School mums were a perfect source of gossip, news, opinion and generally ten times better than Facebook with their speculation. If she could hide in plain sight and listen in, she might find out something of interest to the case.

13.

On a regular Sunday morning, the clique of friends would find themselves, along with many of their neighbours and townspeople down at the Rugby Club. At least, for the friends, they would send the men to spend their mornings there, whilst the women took advantage of empty houses, lie-ins and attempting to recover from their hangovers. Occasionally, for prize giving celebrations or a big advertised match, all the families would get together at the club, and of course, that would lead on to lunch and afternoon drinks. The club was just a stones' throw from the river Ketch. Normally a stunning location, not too far away from the town centre, but surrounded by the beauty of the hills, the river and hectares of green space. The Rugby Club was a hub for social activity and summer picnics.

However, on this Sunday morning, there was so much police activity in the immediate vicinity that it would be impossible for the focus to remain on the games and training going on. Parents who wouldn't have known what had happened on Friday night would naturally be spending their time trying to find out, searching for information and clues. Their kids didn't need to know what had happened, but there was no way they could be out on the pitches oblivious to the actions around them, and so Wayne put a message out to cancel Rugby for Sunday morning. He was up and awake early though, and with nothing else to do, whilst his own kids were enjoying not having to get up, and his wife was still in bed, he sent another message out to the guys on his WhatsApp group to get together for breakfast and try and comprehend what the fuck had happened to their friend. Wayne was probably the most sensitive of the guys in their group. He was generally the one to contact the others, checking in on his friend's if he thought one of them was acting quieter than usual. He would send messages of well-wishes to those under the weather and greetings for birthdays and anniversaries. Generally, it would be Wayne who reached out for anything that wasn't a night out on the piss. The others valued him for that, and they knew he would be the one to turn to if any of them, at a time of distress, could bring themselves to step out of the macho bravado image they wore almost constantly and bare their souls. That didn't happen very often at all though.

But on this Sunday morning, they were all grateful for the intervention and so by 10 o'clock, Richard, Simon, Wayne, Patrick, Lee and Mike were sitting in the Weatherspoons pub, this time drinking coffee with their full English breakfasts. The atmosphere was strained, quiet, the shock still so prominent on all their faces. Lee broke the silence first "Me and Dicky have already been to the police station to give statements. This is so fucked up! I still don't believe that he's actually dead. That he was found lying in the river. What the fuck?" He paused to sip his coffee before continuing "This is Billy we're talking about; loud, brash Billy who never took any shit off anyone, even if he was fond of handing it out a bit too much." There were a few smirks in the group. They all knew that Billy wasn't scared to share his own opinion often and to his enjoyment at the great expense of others, Billy didn't mind who he offended, and everyone knew it. "Do you remember when Billy told that little kid Freddy's Dad that if he ran up the side-line one more time to tell Freddy what he should be doing, and not leaving it to us coaches, he was going to ban him from standing there at all! I don't even know if he was allowed to do that, but he did it in such an aggressive way, and it pissed Freddy's dad off so much he went and sat in his car for the next two weekends, cowering" Wayne reminisced. " I think he even tried to send his wife down to watch him play some weekends because he was shitting himself at home. The man was terrified of Billy." The others started to laugh and more and more stories came out about Billy. There was a time when Billy had persuaded someone at work to sell him their tickets to one of the big matches at Twickenham for less than face value. He convinced the poor man that there was horrendous wind and rain forecast on the day of the match, it would probably be postponed but he might not get his ticket money back or tickets exchanged. He said it so convincingly that the man selling him the tickets was only too happy to get rid of them as quickly as he could. It was safe to say that both the men were quite drunk at the time, enjoying a post work booze up in their Cardiff office. Billy knew that he was talking bullshit, and he also knew that these tickets were being resold online for around £600 a piece. "There was another time", Lee remembered out loud, "when he forgot to tell Cat he was going to Amsterdam for the weekend with some work friends. Do you remember guys, he'd packed his weekend bag, and taken his passport to work with him, but left the house before she had gotten up in the morning, so she was totally unaware of his plans. He only remembered as he was heading for City Airport that afternoon and she had texted him, asking him if he wanted rice or potatoes with his dinner. He texted her back only when he arrived at his hotel in Amsterdam, a few hours later, saying 'don't bother about making me dinner, I'll be back Sunday night'. Poor Cat had tried to call him but his phone rang out, the distinctive overseas ringtone, like an unpleasant buzzing reverberating inside her head. She told Marie that she had spent the weekend planning on leaving him, but never did follow through with her plans".

"Wow, he really did have the balls to do what the hell he wanted" Mike muttered.

"He was so pleased with himself when he told me" Lee sounded quite angry. Mike nodded "How the fuck he got away with it for so long? And did you ever see the amount of porn he had on his phone? Like he didn't care who saw it on there. But if he had a long commute home from the office, he wasn't going to sit there and watch an episode of Game of fucking Thrones!" They laughed at the audacity of their friend.

"I nearly fucking killed him myself once," Richard jumped in, not realising the significance of his choice of words "He told me he was sure Nat was on one of his porn sites. I told him to shut up, but he wouldn't stop going on about her and her fantastic tits that could suffocate a guy, how dirty she was and he tried to go into detail telling me the things she was doing with those tits and another bitch online. Definitely not something you should be watching on public transport is it? And I was so pissed off that he kept on saying she looked just like Nat. He wouldn't fucking shut up! Seriously, I wanted to punch his fucking lights out there and then, but he started laughing and told me to chill out. I had to walk away. I was so pissed off." Richard had turned red under the collar as he spoke. The other men looked at him. They weren't laughing now, they were all thinking the same thing. Richard's choice of words were poor in the given circumstance. Did he mean to use them? Had Billy really made him that mad? Could Richard have killed Billy? He looked so angry, even now sitting in the pub. Did he have it in him to do that? No one wanted to hear their friends talking about their wives like that, but Richard was fuming as he told his story, veins popping up in his forehead and on his neck. Nobody commented on Richard's outburst.

As more and more stories flooded out over the breakfast table, the realisation of Billy's true character was making a bigger appearance. The laughs from the fonder memories were outweighed by Billy's less desirable side. "He was a complete and utter bastard to poor Cat, wasn't he?" Patrick asked. "I mean, none of us would dare talk to our wives the way he did to her! I certainly wouldn't, I'd be fucking petrified she'd hang me up by my balls and swing me around for everyone to have a go at with the cricket bat! Cat put up with so much shit. Fi couldn't understand why she did, to be honest, Fi didn't like Billy much, but you know she's over sensitive and doesn't like the way he disagreed with most of the things she said, just to wind her up!" the guys agreed with him.

"He was so competitive with his kids at Rugby too, wasn't he? Did you see the time Ned was in tears because he missed a try and Billy came down on him like a ton of bricks, in front of all the other kids too," Simon contributed. "He would always play his kids too, knowing there were others that might have had a better game that week. I mean, I do understand that in a way, what with all the effort he put into coaching the kids. There must be some advantage sometimes of all that unpaid hard work, and his kids are both amazing Rugby players. Except do you remember this one time he put Jason on after he'd twisted his ankle and took my Oscar off. Both kids were in tears for the whole morning. Jason was in absolute agony, Oscar was heartbroken. He'd been having a brilliant game that day! I wanted to say something to Billy, but the look on his face when I walked over to him told me to let it go."

Simon's son Oscar was best friends with Jason. They had grown up together from nursery days and were in the same class at school. Jason would often go to Simon and Jaycee's to play after school whilst Ned was at one sports club or another and Billy and Cat were both at work. Simon was fond of Jason, but at times he could see how demanding he was, just like his father. "He's a good kid, is Jason, but boy has he got his father's temperament! On several occasions" he continued, "Jaycee had to step in before a fight broke out between the two boys. Jason would demand that Oscar give him one of his toys and literally pocket it to take home. He would also mandate his food order to Jaycee and refuse the foods he didn't want to eat. Again, I wouldn't do that myself to Jay. She would tell me where to go anyway. Jaycee used to say to me, 'He's his father's son' and we would laugh it off and then agree for him to come over the next time, never mentioning it to Cat or Bill". None of them had ever mentioned Jason's behaviour to Billy for fear of him getting angry and forceful, and no one dared say anything to Cat for fear of upsetting her any more than she already was and so they pretended it wasn't happening, and let it continue. Simon was good friends with Billy, all the men were, but Billy was certainly not one of his favourites.

It hadn't gone amiss the times that Simon and Jaycee had hosted parties and Billy had overly flirted with Jaycee. Jaycee had never shown any attention back to Billy and quite often would move out of his reach when he came into a room she was in. Simon could see that Billy pissed his wife off, but she was so polite and such a good host that she preferred to avoid a situation rather than speak her mind, or allow his behaviour to get to her. Unlike some of the other wives, thought Simon, who obviously enjoyed the little extra attention. Simon glanced up at Richard, wondering if he was aware of what his wife was capable of. Maybe not internet porn, but she wasn't as innocent as she liked to make out.

Patrick nodded in agreement. "He did put his boys on a pedestal out on the field, didn't he?" The others muttered their agreement too. "Do you know," Mike added "the fucker never gave me the money back for our last ski trip! Jen was on at me to ask him for it, because she didn't want to cause a scene with Cat. I must have mentioned it to him about 4 times and he always said 'Yeah of course mate, I'll sort it as soon as I get home' and promptly forgot. But then whenever he booked tickets for something, we certainly were made sure to pay him up front before he got them, weren't we?" Mike looked visibly pissed off as he was telling the guys. Mike was a hard worker and probably earned the least out of the group of friends. They planned their annual ski trips as a no-expense spared luxury, and it was always a conscious effort for Mike to put the money aside to pay for it. He had been reluctant to pay out for Billy when Billy had asked him, but he also didn't want his best friend missing out and he knew that Billy earned good money and could easily pay him back. Throughout the five day holiday, Mike had been subconsciously aware of everything Billy spent in the bars, restaurants and he knew that the one night Billy didn't go back to the chalet with them hadn't been a freebie either. Billy wasn't short of a few bob, but he didn't like to put his hand in his own pocket. Mike hadn't mentioned it to the other guys at the time, he thought they would take piss out of him and call him out for being stingy or broke. Mike and Jen had recently inherited their decent sized home from her father who had passed away from cancer, but who had made sure that his only daughter would be looked after considerably well on her own after he was gone. The bills for the house alone would have equated to the cost of a mortgage if they'd had to have bought the house on loan, so they knew they were lucky to have the house gifted to them, with money aside for the inheritance tax too. However that all came at a heavier price than the previous terraced house they had lived in in Molville and they were having to adjust their spend to make sure they could cover it, without looking like they were struggling.

"He did put himself on a bit of a pedestal too" Lee added, "a bit of an Animal Farm fan perhaps 'All men are equal but Billy is more equal than others'" he laughed. "Come on, let's toast to Billy. It may only be coffee, but we'll have a lot more opportunities to toast him with what he loved best later! To Billy!" All the men raised their coffee cups "A total fucking wanker but he was our mate and we loved him and boy will we miss him!" Lee wiped a tear away with his sleeve and he hoped no one else had noticed.

The men finished up in the pub and made their separate ways home, to take over child duties and give their wives some time to go and spend with Cat. Mixed emotions as they left the pub, each of them deep in thought about the impact Billy had had on their own lives.

Jen, Mike's wife, phoned Cat early that Sunday afternoon. They chatted for a while but Jen was extremely nervous to know the right things to say. She wasn't the greatest conversationalist and hated forced situations where she had to pretend to know what was the best thing to do and what to avoid. Cat could sense her awkwardness and tried to guide the conversation, despite not knowing what she was doing herself. Eventually Jen dropped into the conversation that all the women were free to go over and spend time with Cat later that day, but she wasn't sure if she should offer to bring the prosecco or if it would be a tea kind of afternoon. She put the ball in Cat's court "So do you want us over or would you rather be with your parents?" she offered. Cat immediately replied, relieved that she had finally said what Cat was waiting to hear, with "Come now, and bring the bottles, I'm not coping very well sober at the moment ". Jen heaved a massive sigh of relief. That was a deal. 3pm was never too early to start drinking and Jen, pleased with her progress, called the other girls and arranged to meet at Cat's that afternoon.

Natalya still wasn't sure if she was up to moving around, she was still in agony and in no mood to go out, but she really didn't want to miss out on being with her friends. Her guilty conscience had her thinking that the others would be talking about her. She couldn't take that risk of them all being together whilst she stayed at home and so she had to make an effort to show a strong front of support for Cat, and keep everyone else quiet. She wasn't stupid and she knew what happened behind closed doors, about the gossip and bitching. It didn't matter how close the friends were, she knew from first hand experience, as she was always first to start a new rumour about someone else, constantly going out of her way to hunt it down, and at this time she couldn't afford to be the subject of their talk. Richard however, couldn't understand why she was trying to manoeuvre herself off the couch. "They'll manage without you" he said to her as she winced in pain in an effort to crawl up the stairs to put some makeup on and get changed. "No, I need to be there to support my friend, " she snapped back. "She needs me. She's a mourning widow! Do you not understand?" "But all the other girls will be there, they can look after her, and you can spend all your time with her when you're feeling stronger," he argued. But no, Natalya put her foot down, gingerly, and crawled up the stairs to find her loosest pair of trousers to feel most comfortable in. In the end she settled for a pair of stretch jeggings, which were pure agony to put on and a long jumper to ensure the tops of her legs were well and truly covered over. Her legs were in agony, but she wasn't prepared to share the reason why to her friends just yet. She had wanted to wait until she was fully recovered to do that. She hoped that a few glasses of prosecco would numb the pain a bit. But stopped her bravery at walking to Cat's house though, despite only living one road away, and as gracefully as she could, accepted a lift from Richard.

14.

Cat managed to put on her full face of makeup to welcome her friends over. Her father couldn't understand why she was preening herself when her husband had just died but her mother knew the importance of trying to look her best, especially in such a disaster, especially when she was going to be the centre of attention, even if it was only from your girlfriends. She opened a few bags of crisps and took out the glasses from the cupboard.

Natalya was the first to arrive and Cat surveyed her closely as she watched her friend hobble in. "What have you done?" she asked. "Oh just a pulled muscle" Natalya limped in. Cat didn't believe her one bit, there was definitely something more that she was hiding, and she would eventually find out when her mind was a little clearer. "I'll be fine if I just rest a bit, I'm going to park myself on your sofa and not move if you don't mind, " Natalya added. As always, her focus was purely about herself, no thought to anyone else around her, and she wasn't open to any other suggestions either.

Cat didn't mind. She was used to being 2nd in command, following up the rear. She could also see that her friend was really struggling, so she would let it go for now. She waved goodbye to Richard, as he turned the car around in her driveway and shut the door behind Natalya, guiding her into the kitchen. Her parents and the kids had decided to camp out in the front room for the rest of the day. They had snacks, the TV and one of the games consoles and she knew that they wouldn't interrupt her and her friends. She needed this time to not have to put a brave face on. The others all arrived within 10 minutes of each other and Claire, as always, took over the responsibility of pouring the drinks and putting the snacks on the table. There were awkward hugs and mutters of condolences from Jen and Fiona, who hadn't yet had a chance to speak to Cat. Jaycee had brought flowers too and busied herself with finding a vase to put them in. No one noticed that Natalya hadn't got up to help fuss around. She wasn't known to be the most forthcoming and helpful of the friends and was happy for once that her selfishness meant she wouldn't be questioned. "It's a shame Marie isn't here" Jaycee noticed as she did a silent headcount of the group.

"Oh she's still in Yarmouth" Cat answered. " Back later tonight, but she did call me yesterday and we must have chatted for about an hour".

Marie was the kindest, probably most genuine member of the group. She always knew what to say at the right time, always there as a shoulder to cry on but never forcing her way into someone else's private life. She was never the subject of anyone's gossip, because she wore her heart on her sleeve. If she disagreed with something, she said so, and the others would have no choice but to agree or accept her opinion. She was also the first to compliment any of the others, she was never jealous of how anyone looked or what they wore, she was genuinely just a really nice person. They all had the utmost respect for Marie and raised a glass to her in her absence.

The drinks were served by Claire and with all the fussing of arrivals done, the women sat down, suddenly a heavy silence hanging over them all. The silence was broken by Fiona. "Fuck" she said quite loudly and very clearly, "Fuck, I'm so so sorry Cat. I don't know what to say, I don't know what to do."

"That's ok" Cat replied, "I understand. I think I just want to talk as we normally would. Tell me all what you've been up to this weekend? Take my mind off this horrific shit. I can start us off. I went out for drinks with Lauren and Tracy on Friday because none of you were around. We went to the Dog and Duck, but Lauren wasn't really drinking because she had to be up at stupid o'clock on Saturday to take Harry to somewhere like Stevenage for a game. It was nice though. We even got a table for a change."

"Any goss?" Jen jumped in without thinking. Although she wasn't one to socialise much outside her own group of friends, she always wanted to know what was going on with everyone else. Fi frowned at her, but they all turned to Cat, hoping to start a conversation about others not in their group. It alleviated a lot of guilt.

"No, not really." Cat replied calmly. "We were talking about secondary schools and when we'll find out where the boys are going. But Lauren doesn't really mind and Tracey lives so close to that new one, she's happily convinced herself that's what he'll get. We did talk about planning the year 6 leavers' party too. There is so much stuff to do, and we ought to allocate tasks to people. I told them that you guys would all help me with decorating the venue and liaising with the DJ. Tracy said that Ellen was offering to help loads too, but she's such an annoying, nosy cow. I can't stand her, the little witch!"

Ellen was another Mum at school. Her daughter was friend's with some of their children and Ellen was also good friends with Marie. But Ellen and Cat clashed and had done so ever since Ellen took on the role of class rep in Reception and continued in that role throughout the whole of primary school. Ellen was one of those people who wanted to be friends with everyone, but also had a penchant for sharing the gossip too, and speaking her mind, which pissed off those who might have had something to hide.

"Ellen's not that bad really," Fiona added. "I think she just feels really left out because she's not one of us. She tries hard doesn't she? You can see the way she always looks over at us, desperate for an invitation, but her husband obviously doesn't like any of us! So he can do one, as far as I care" she chuckled.

"I can't think why!" Claire joined in sarcastically "But she's an opinionated bitch, who likes to do her own thing all the time anyway. I don't want her taking over the leavers' party. She'll put her dirty paw prints all over it and then wait for all the recognition to come flooding in on her smug stupid face. She'd probably insist we only drink juice because it's a kids party and will make stupid party bags for the kids to take home. Urgh, I'll have to get really involved now!" Claire looked quite angry.

"Well, we all know about yours and her little spat" Jen laughed. "She's good with the kids though and my girls and hers get on really well. Anyway, Ellen or no Ellen, we need to start thinking about the leavers' party then. A good heads up, thanks Cat!"

The women carried on talking about the other mothers from the year group. It was always fun to dissect them and rate them. There was the drippy Mum who didn't let her daughter go to anyone's house without tagging along herself. None of the mum's particularly liked her and as a result her daughter had the fewest playdates of anyone they knew. There was the snorty mum, who obviously had a little problem with coke on the dashboard of her car, before picking up her son from school and there was the mum whose daughter was destined for a future in TV, but most probably Love Island or something just as derogatory. They talked about how the families had changed in the 7 years they had been at the school, which families had split up and how it was so unsurprising. " You couldn't have a more mismatched couple than Sasha's parents" Jaycee said "You know her mum denied it for almost two years, and Sasha wasn't allowed to mention it in school but then told all her friends anyway when they were on the coach going up to London on their last trip. Apparently all the other kids responded with a 'whatever!'. Shame her mum shuts it away. She could really get some support if she just accepted it. Sasha's ok though. Oscar said she's acted no different since the split, isn't upset and gets a lot of presents from her Dad. Quite a nice kid really". Some of the others nodded.

"Has drab Denise been on the phone to you yet Cat?" asked Fiona "she's even nosier than Ellen. I'll bet she wants to know exactly what's happened, where and when. You never know she might even do a better detective job than the police." Fiona stopped talking, worried that she'd overstepped the mark again. But Cat laughed "I'm fully expecting her call or at least a text, but surprisingly she's not been in touch. I'll tell Ned to watch out for her daughter at school tomorrow, you can guarantee she'll be under instructions to draw any information out of my poor son." The laugh left her face, "It's going to be awful walking in tomorrow, but I hope once I've done it the first time, people should back off."

"I will take the boys in," Claire offered. "You really don't need to face everyone until you're ready. Don't rush into it. Don't even send the boys in if you don't want to. Make sure they are ready before they go back, but if and when they are, we can all do rota's to get them there and safely home again." The others nodded in agreement. Cat thanked them and slowly the conversation turned round to Billy.

"Who would do this to him? And why?" Cat asked rhetorically. It left the others contemplating quietly to themselves, but Jaycee couldn't help but look over at Natalya, sitting curled up on the couch. She knew Natalya had something to hide, but now wasn't the time or place to bring it up. She wanted to catch her eye though, and let her know that she knew. Natalya sat quietly, desperately trying not to show any emotion other than the one for the loss of her friend's husband. She daren't look at anyone else but could sense eyes bearing down on her. She straightened her shoulders and back, trying to sit as tall and confidently as she could, but kept her eyes down avoiding any direct contact.

Fiona, again with less tact than the others, couldn't help but break the silence. "Do you think it was someone we know? Someone he knew?" she asked. "I mean, we all loved Billy of course, but he was a dickhead at times. Oh god, sorry. I've done it again. Should I leave?" She hung her head and went to get up.

"No, don't go. Please." Said Cat, reaching out to her friend. "I know you only mean well. You're probably just saying what everyone else is thinking! I loved Billy, but he wasn't the nicest of people. To me and to others." She looked around at her friends. "I know he was a bully and I know he loved looking at other women. I hated that so much. He would actually watch porn on his phone on the train coming home from work! He thought I never knew, but I did. I wouldn't even be surprised if he'd been screwing around behind my back. I mean, all those work trips he took, and the way he pushed me aside far too often." She looked around the room as she said this, her eyes resting slightly longer on Natalya as she did. "Thinking out loud, there is no way he wasn't doing it. What the hell did I put up with all that time?"

Natalya wanted to run out of the room and cry. Thanks to being in agony though she couldn't get up and move away. Surely Cat didn't know about her and Billy. She wouldn't have invited her into her home if she did, would she?

"I think I want to hear the bad stuff from you lot too if you've got any," continued Cat. "Today I want to hate him for leaving me. Maybe tomorrow I'll regret this, but today" she poured herself another large glass of prosecco and went around the room filling up the other glasses, "Today I want him to be a bastard and I can get drunk with my friends and be angry. So please, speak your minds. Tell me what an arse he was. I need you to!"

Everyone looked back to Fiona, as she was the most insensitive of them all. "Why me?" she looked back at them all. And without a second thought she started the ball rolling. "Well, I know he was quite mean to some of the Rugby Dads, and when I say quite mean, I mean he was really nasty. I know he threatened one of them once, for trying to give a bit of coaching advice to his own son. And yeah, he was a perv. He asked me once if I was wearing a bra under my top and asked if he could check. My god he was pissed that day. I told him where to go though, cheeky fucker! To be honest though, I've always got on quite well with him. We used to have a good laugh together. I'll stop now, I can't add anything more, sorry."

Jen piped up next. "He never paid Mike for their last skiing trip. Mike was pretty pissed off about that!"

"Oh my god, why didn't you tell me?" asked Cat. "I'll transfer the money right away".

"No, don't be stupid. Don't do that. It was between Mike and Billy. If Mike didn't have the balls to beat it out of him, then that's Mike's loss". There was no way Jen was going to take anything from her friend. Especially as she knew if it had been the other way round, Billy wouldn't bail her out at all.

Claire added her two pence worth next "He was quite rude to me to be honest. I don't know if it was because he was jealous of me, or of the relationship I have with Wayne . Billy was over flirty with you girls and others. He must have sensed that I would never give in to his flirting, as Wayne and I are so tight together, and not that I ever wanted him to, but sometimes when we were having a conversation, and not even a flirty one" she quickly added, "he would quite obviously turn his head the other way to watch someone else and whatever they were doing and completely ignore me!"

"Oh that's my Billy for sure" Cat said. "He used to do that to me all the time. Bloody rude actually" she giggled, topping up her glass again. Claire was relieved that she had put her point across and didn't have to think of anything else. She had made a clear statement that he was a flirt, but she would never rise to the challenge, unlike some of her other friends. Deep down she was still seething. If he was known to be such a slut, such a womaniser, why the hell had he used her up and spat her out like a piece of gristle when she had desperately offered herself on a plate. Billy had been her challenge, her project and her determination, but now she had failed as he had snubbed her at almost every corner, except when he wanted something purely for his own pleasure.

"Cat, tell us more about Billy," Fi said. "We talk about what a wanker he is, but do we know or even want to know who has done this or why?" She wasn't sure if she was digging a big hole for herself but couldn't seem to stop. "Did he have enemies? I mean real enemies? What about you, Cat?" She sniggered, thinking that clean Cat wouldn't have anyone who wanted their revenge on her.

"I just don't know," Cat replied, looking a bit forlorn. "I mean, he pissed people off, we all know that. But who hasn't? I don't know about anyone at work because he never told me. To be honest, I don't know much about his past either! We generally didn't talk about our histories. I know he's had a past, but I never wanted to know in detail".

"I bet he slept with hundreds of girls when he was younger!" Fi was being completely tactless again. "Oh shit, too much again" she apologised.

"So maybe it's YOUR past then," joked Jen, trying to join in a bit more. "Maybe it's a jilted lover who is trying to win you back!"

They all laughed, all of them except for Cat, who brushed them off with a "yeah likely" comment as she put an end to that conversation. Her past was in the past and not even her closest friends needed to be privy to it. Time to take the focus off herself.

Cat looked around at her friends again. She needed to know if Natalya had slept with her husband but was she brave enough to ask her outright in front of the others? "Come on, lets have more dirt" she said to the group, turning back to Natalya "Nat, you must have something on him too," she directed the conversation, happy that should it backfire she could blame it on the Prosecco.

"Me? Why me?" Natalya felt an immediate knot in her stomach but realised that they were just going around the room, and she had to join in. "Well, what can I say? He and Dicky were quite competitive and he would often undermine Dicky if he could, especially down at the club. I don't know what else to say though!" she thought she had gotten away without mentioning anything of any importance.

"Really?" Cat couldn't stop herself. "Is that all? What about you and Billy? How was *your* relationship with him?"

Natalya wanted to hide, but she had to hold herself up and stay strong. She was the only one who knew about her and Billy, and now Billy was dead, she could deny anything thrown at her. "Well he did once comment on the length of my dress, something about only wearing a T-shirt, but I told him to piss off." She said, ``I really don't have anything else to say about him though"

Jaycee spluttered, almost spilling her prosecco. "I really thought he had a thing for you Nat" she added. "Do you remember a few months ago at my house when he was following you around like a lost puppy?"

"No, I don't remember that." Natalya answered, too quickly for her own good.

"Yes, when you were in that Tshirt dress you just mentioned. He had his eye on you all night. It was pretty obvious, wasn't it Claire?"

Claire nodded in agreement.

Natalya was saved having to respond by Cat's phone ringing. It was Marie to see how she was getting on, and to make sure Cat knew, even though she was far away, she was thinking of her. Cat chatted to her for a few minutes which halted the current conversation topic. "That's so lovely of Marie to call" Natalya quickly tried to change the subject. The other's agreed and they acknowledged the change in banter into something much more friendly. They all knew they were treading on dangerous ground and although Cat was enjoying the chance to slate her dead husband today, she might completely change her mind tomorrow and resent her friend's words from today.

When Cat got off the phone from Marie, the women had moved back to talking about the year 6 leaver's party again, and plans for a leavers photo book and hoodies too. The women stayed for a while longer before making their excuses to get home and get their kids ready for school the next day. Cat made the decision after briefly talking to her own children that she wanted to send them to school, to give them a distraction. Claire bossily told Cat that she would swing by in the morning to pick her boys up whilst Jaycee and Jen cleared up the empty bottles, putting the glasses in the dishwasher and generally tidying up. only Natalya again didn't move off the couch.

Although the drink had numbed her pain considerably, she didn't want to risk the other's seeing her move like John Wayne. She would wait until the others had left before calling Richard to pick her up again.

15.

On Monday morning, Carly woke early and spent some time, with a steaming hot coffee from her new Nespresso machine, examining her wall of suspects. She hadn't stopped thinking about the Facebook message and the wording for the best part of her Sunday afternoon and evening. She had logged calls and was waiting for feedback from IT but she knew there was more that she could be doing in the meantime. She needed to find more clues to the whole case, and was still waiting for the rest of the CCTV footage of Billy's supposed journey home to come back to her. She hadn't contacted Billy's work yet but wanted to check in with her boss before doing so. Carly was generally quite patient, but she didn't want to sit around waiting on all the information due back to her. She decided that in the interim, she would take a stroll up to the school playground to see what she could find out there. Probably best to go plain clothes she thought, otherwise the mum's might not feel comfortable gossiping in front of a uniformed officer. Although not a mother herself, Carly was well aware of the school gate activities. She knew that mothers were catagorised into various different groupings that defined their level of hierarchy, importance, gossip and many other gradings. Often the Mums were worse than the children. She also knew that the film Bad Moms wasn't a million miles away from real life with some of these schools.

She called her boss to tell him of her plan. "Do you want me to speak to his office?" she asked DI Sidhu. "No, I can do that, I might take a trip up to London and scope out the place too. I'm happy for you to do the school run, you'll fit in much better than me. Carly, you know what I need you to do and I have every faith that you will do an amazing job of it."

She would need to interview some of the teaching staff too in order to understand if the Ashton children had shown any change in personality, talked about any problems or anything else that was out of the norm, in the run up to their father's death. She called Daniel and told him of her plan, and that she would go up initially on her own, to blend in easier with the busy mum's. Of course, she might arrive there to find a playground full of Dads and grandparents. She wasn't completely sexist, but she was willing to take the risk of it being predominantly the mothers at the gate. But with Daniel there, two of them standing in the playground with no children might look a bit conspicuous. Daniel agreed and was happy not to have to go up to the school. He was planning to go into the station and chase up the CCTV and IT requests they were waiting on. They arranged a time to meet back at the station later in the morning.

Carly got herself ready, thinking how she could blend in the most, it was an easy choice of blue jeggings, a knitted jumper and her uggs. She drove the relatively short distance to the boys school and parked her civilian car around the corner, already blending in with the other mother's, parking their huge 4 by 4's wherever they could, ignoring the road signs and markings trying to prevent them from parking exactly where they had stopped their cars. Signs that could save their children from getting run over, and blocking the clear view of the Lollipop Lady who tirelessly smiled at all the children, and frowned at all the drivers. Carly stopped for a moment to witness cars speeding up to within feet of the poor woman standing in the middle of the road. The problem with the world was that people had no patience any more. they expected to do what they want and when they wanted to, but why did they not slow down near a school and near an elderly lady in a high-vis jacket and a flipping huge lollipop, that was still beyond her. She shuddered and made a mental note to mention to her PCSO to go and check on another day. There were no rules around the school run, they obviously didn't count if you were only staying for 10 minutes. Maybe she would be the same if she got married and had kids, but she couldn't see herself being a traffic rule breaker, let alone any other type of rule breaker. That went against all her beliefs and values as an aspiring future police detective. She carried on her journey through the school gates and into the playground.

It was a hive of activity in the playground and Carly was happy that she could blend in without any difficulty, as her previous thought was correct, it was predominantly females hanging around the playground chatting away to each other. Luckily the Year 6 area was near the front entrance of the school and she didn't have to walk across the tarmac, without a child, to hang around the other parents.

She heard her first piece of news within seconds of arriving and set her mind to memorise everything she was hearing, as there was no way she would be able to write any of this down. An extremely loud mother, not one she recognised from Billy or Cat's Facebook pages was talking to another unrecognised woman "I can't believe there has been a murder in Oldcoeswood" she said. "Bloody awful isn't it, in our little town? Those poor Ashton kids too. Can't imagine what they must be going through" Carly made a mental picture of the woman speaking and moved slightly away to another small group of women, with more hushed tones to their voices. She just about heard their conversation "You did hear that Billy has apparently been murdered?" a short woman was saying to the other two. "I mean, he's a complete bastard but who would wish that on anyone?" Carly stood as close as she could without being obvious. There was some information to be gained from this conversation. Picture building for her wall at home.

"Well I saw on Facebook that the poor rubbish guy found him naked in the stream. Do you think it was a dodgy sex game gone wrong?" another added. The other two women sniggered.

"Sex game with who though?" the first woman asked "Not Cat, for sure! He was such a spiteful misogynist and treated her like absolute shit. I don't know why she stuck with him." her voice lowered noticeably. "She told me once, when she was really pissed on a mum's night out, and we were pretending that we liked each other, how he had thrown a plate of dinner in the bin, despite her having cooked after she herself had worked all day, because he didn't like the look of it. ! Oh, do you think she killed him?"

"Oh Ellen, no it wouldn't have been her" The third woman contributed. "She wouldn't have done that. She's way too soft. She literally let him walk all over her. Remember when she told us about how he used to actually push her out of the way, and he would go to the bar to get himself a drink but not get her one. What a shit. But you know he was shagging Natalya don't you? Everyone knew that. It's so bloody obvious. I think the only people who didn't know were Richard and Cat! Unless they were all sharing each other. But I don't think Cat would." She stopped for a breath.

Carly was desperately storing the information she had just come across, mentally putting it on post-it notes on the wall by the photograph of Natalya. This was pure Gold dust, and she was proud of herself for coming up to the school that morning. Of course none of the information she was hearing was verified but it was all clues to take forward to the next stage. She subtly switched her phone on to record, just in case she missed any of this valuable data.

"Oh Jean, you're such a gossip" the second woman said turning to face the third woman who had mentioned Natalya "we don't actually know that for sure, do we? There isn't actually proof anywhere. But I agree, he wasn't very nice. He completely ignored my Jack once when Jack was with Ned and Billy came to collect his son. Jack said hello to him as he walked over to them both and he literally ignored him and started speaking to Ned. No other parent has ever done that to my Jack, and you know he likes to pretend he's one of the adults when speaking to them. They always respond and chat back to him. It's what makes his day."

"He's a bastard Harriet, how could he be so rude to Jack. Jack is so polite" Ellen said. "Poor Jack" She continued to compliment her friend's son and Carly decided that they weren't going to go back to talking about Billy, especially as Ned and Jason had just walked into the playground with one of Cat's friends. Claire, Carly guessed right. She stood back to watch the change in atmosphere and activity. Claire took the two boys straight into the school building. She wasn't going to hang around the playground for them to be stared at. The two boys looked quite scared as they went in with her arms around both their shoulders and her own son lagging behind. It was time for Carly to go and talk to the head teacher and leave the playground gossip for another time.

She spent quite a while with the most helpful head teacher she had ever come across. This was a woman who not only knew every single child in her school, but knew the parents, the grandparents, the carers and everything else. Whilst she did remain very reserved with giving her personal opinion of the family, she did give the impression that there was a very close knit social clique of parents, of which Billy had been a firm member of. She was able to confirm the other parents Carly suggested but would not offer any speculation on anyone. It was back to Facebook for Carly, but she was quite confident she had a good understanding of Billy's closest friends and would continue with her interviews of them all back at the station. She thanked the Head Teacher profusely for her time and information, again mentally placing her post-it notes onto the wall as she left the premises.

Whilst Carly was at the school, in receipt of some quite valuable information, her boss DI Sidhu had put an urgent call in to the Insurance company that Billy had worked at. It hadn't taken him long to get the phone number of the CEO's personal assistant and just after 8am he was on the phone to a pleasant enough sounding lady by the name of Louise Crofter. After introducing himself and explaining that it was inevitable he speak to her boss as soon as possible with regards to Billy Ashton, he was put through to the CEO.

Steven Grey was an abrupt man, and didn't seem to want to spend much time on the phone to James, and so James decided that he would grace him and the rest of the office with a visit, much to Steven's irritation. Steven tried to imply that he was far too busy, but no one was too busy for a murder case, and James headed straight off to the train station to get the first train to Paddington.

On arrival at the offices, James showed his badge to a frightened looking young girl at reception. He tried to ease her fear by smiling and chatting. Everyone he came into contact with was either a suspect or a source of information, and years of practicing his career had taught him that the receptionist was someone to get as close as possible to. They saw much more than everyone else. Lydia Young, an attractive straight out of school would-be model had been at the company for almost a year. She had definitely been put at the front of the company purely for her looks. A head turner for sure. Despite her fear, she called up to Steven Grey and James was given instructions on how to find him on the first floor.

The meeting with Steven was not overly productive. Steven confirmed that Billy had worked for the company for over 10 years, and was a senior broker. He was a good salesman and secured a lot of repeat business for the company. Because of his dedication and the amount of money brought in, Steven did admit that a blind eye was often turned to some of Billy's antics. "What sort of antics?" James was writing down everything he heard. "Oh nothing too drastic," Steven answered. "Maybe his bedside manner could have been improved a little. He received a few complaints especially from the graduates, who he may have treated a little unfairly. He wanted to introduce an initiation process, but I put a stop to that. Our initiation process as he so calls it is for us to look at suitable CV's and then interview the best candidates, no drinking games and dares." Steven didn't show any emotion as he carried on. "Of course, everyone relaxes a little more at staff events, and Billy was no exception", he coughed a little nervously.
"Go on," James encouraged.

"Well, there was an incident about two years ago when one of the previous receptionists claimed that he sexually assaulted her in his hotel room. Nothing was proven at the time, it was her word against his and by the time he'd argued his case to me and the rest of the senior team, she had resigned and we heard nothing further about it."

"I will need to take down her name and contact details please" James added. "Did the case ever get to the police?"

"No, nothing like that. In fact, I recall Billy apologised to Debbie for what he might have misread into their relationship and then it all settled down."

"Except she felt that she had to resign!" James exclaimed.

"Well, she was planning to go travelling, and I think that seemed as good a time as any for her to set off." Steven started to look uncomfortable.

"Has Billy had a 'relationship' with anyone else here?" James continued. Keen to paint a complete picture of his womanising victim.

"You know," Steven added reluctantly. "We are quite a young company here, we have a lot of social events and they are always alcohol fueled. What the youngsters do outside of their working hours is really none of my business. I don't go on all the jolly's and so Billy usually takes charge and takes the company card with him. As long as no one posts anything on social media, they are all responsible adults in my opinion."

Having gained a greater insight into Billy's work, James requested some time with Louise Crofter next. She was much friendlier than her boss, and offered James a hot drink before they sat down to talk. She was happy to speak her mind about Billy. "He was such a womaniser" she started off, "ever since I've been at the company, which is about 5 years now, he's tried it on with me at every opportunity. Even though he's met my partner, Sophie, who I've been with for years." She huffed. "He just couldn't leave me alone, and would suggest coming home to video me and her. I mean, what a sicko, right?" James listened intently. "I thought it was just banter, and was happy to tell him where to get off. I'm not going to start complaining about him, because he was so much more senior than me and I love working here, I wasn't going to jeopardise my job for a dickhead like Billy. So sorry sir, I shouldn't talk ill of the dead like that, should I?"

"Please, keep going," James encouraged her. "Your opinion is so valuable to us right now."

"So me and Soph stopped going to the socials when we knew that he was going to be there, and it was odd that even at the parties where partners were invited, he never brought his wife with him. I knew he was married but I didn't know much about her. Maybe they've split up. It wouldn't surprise me because he never went back to a hotel alone. Dirty bugger. He literally would pounce on all the younger women as soon as they joined the company. We have a great graduate programme here, so we get lots of kids, as I like to call them, join each year, and he spends much more time getting to know the girls rather than the guys. Oh my god I've seen so many walks of shame the morning after the night before, if you know what I mean?"

"Can you tell me more about Debbie?" James had made notes of everything that Louise was telling him.

"Oh poor Debbie. Well I didn't know her that well, but I did join the company not long before she left. I was on reception you see, before I got promoted to PA. Debbie did my job before me. She was really lovely. Very shy and didn't know how pretty she really was. So anyway, as he always did, Billy made a move on her when she was quite new to the company apparently. This is what she told me anyway, and the reason she started self-defence classes too. But the night when the shit really hit the fan was at our Summer party two years ago. Me and Soph were taking it easy that night because we were going on holiday the next day, and I can't bear hangovers on a plane, so I stayed relatively sober. Poor Debbie had a few too many though and I actually watched as Billy made a move on her, like a wild animal going in for the kill. He cornered her, and she was giggling quite a lot but then his hands started roaming a little, like in public you know, and she was sort of blushing and I could see that she was a bit embarrassed, so I went over to her to check she was ok. But she said she was and then she did go off again with him. She was single you know, but a bit older, I think she was desperate for a boyfriend. She was nearly 30. So me and Sophie left and I didn't hear anything else until I got back from holiday a week later." Louise stopped to breathe before she continued.

"Anyway, Debbie was off sick for a few days and got back to work around the time I did too. She was really withdrawn though and it took me ages to get her to come to lunch with me. When she did though, the poor thing broke down. She swore me to secrecy so that's why I didn't tell anyone. But basically, she went back to the hotel with Billy and they had sex but he video'd it and then when she was asleep he took photos of her naked. When she went home the next day she felt awful because apparently Billy had talked about his wife a few times, and Debbie doesn't do things like that, so she texted Billy and said it was all a mistake. That's when he told her about the video and pics. Debbie was horrified, you can imagine. Poor cow didn't know what to do. I told her to report it but Billy had already told her if she did he would send the photos viral and he knew some dirty old men who would love to enjoy pics of a naked woman on their screens. Told her what they would do whilst looking at her pictures. So she didn't but then she handed her notice in straight away. She moved to Germany of all places. I think she has an old aunt there or something. I tried to contact her and she did get in touch about a month ago because she was in London and we met up for lunch but she looked so different. So, well plain really. She was wearing really baggy clothes and her hair was cut shorter, she's still pretty but you'd have to look hard to see that now. Such a shame."

Finally Louise stopped talking and James could stop writing. He thanked Louise for her time, and armed with his notes and a phone number for Debbie he headed back down to reception to speak with Lydia once again. As with all the other women, Lydia confessed that she had kissed Billy but hadn't gone back to his hotel with him because her boyfriend was a boxer and very over protective of her. It had been a big mistake but she had convinced Billy to stay away, and insisted her boyfriend come to every social function after that incident.

James headed off back to the station. He was looking forward to catching up with his team that afternoon and putting their facts together so far.

As Carly was leaving the school, also armed with the information she had gained from the other parents and the staff, she had a call from Daniel who was already at the station. Daniel had been chasing up the CCTV and had received further CCTV footage of Billy leaving the pub and more to add to the story. Carly ran to her car, excited about a potential break in her first ever murder case. She was back at the station within 10 minutes and Daniel had already poured her a coffee as he pulled a chair out for her to sit next to him.

The CCTV footage was taken from the middle of the High Street, a different camera to that which followed Lee and Richard walking away from the town centre. This one picked up Billy, 7 minutes after the camera by the pub had lost him. He was on the High Street but strangely walking back in the direction of the pub, and away from his homeward journey. He was walking towards the roundabout that would lead to the river. He looked extremely drunk on the camera, he was swerving all over the pavement, and on a couple of occasions, lost his footing and tripped off the curb onto the road. There was no one else seen in the footage. The streets were otherwise empty. Carly and Daniel continued to watch patiently. They would see it through until Billy was no longer on the screen. After 3 minutes a couple walked past him. They turned and looked at him but continued their walk, arm in arm in the opposite direction. Still, it was worth looking further into them, they might have been the last people to see Billy alive. Them, and his alleged killer. After a further four minutes, when Billy had crossed the traffic lights, still heading towards the river, and now at a right angle to the road that would have taken him back to the pub he started from, a car appeared, driving towards him. This was a one-way street, Billy walking the opposite way to the flow of the traffic. A few cars were parked further down, but this was the only moving vehicle on the screen.

The two police officers looked closely at the car, it was a people carrier. So common in a town like Oldcoewood with four primary schools and God only knows how many nurseries. It was a true family town. But this people carrier looked as if it had caught a stray carrier bag from the gentle wind blowing on that May night. The carrier bag had managed to cover up all but one solid black line of the front number plate as the car drove down the road. Was that a coincidence or a very strategically placed cover-up?

"The driver has stopped," Daniel said out loud, despite everyone in the room giving the screen their full attention. "They've pulled over right next to Billy". All eyes opened just that little bit wider and breathing became quieter. The car had indeed pulled over and they could just make out the window winding down. The driver had a dark hood on, it was near impossible to make out anything about them. Billy stopped and turned to the driver. The CCTV was behind him, so his facial expressions could not be detected. It was clear to see that Billy was still very much wobbling in his drunken state, and he put his hands on the window opening to steady himself. A few seconds later he walked out into the road, and after a couple of attempts, managed to open the passenger door and plant himself in the car with the driver.

That was it. They had their link and a clear view of the car, albeit without a number plate or a distinct colour. It just looked grey in the dark footage of the camera. The time was noted down, a photo printed out of the car and everyone in the room busied themselves with a different task in logging this new and vital piece of information.

Someone else in the room called out that he was looking at the footage from a camera further back down the road, to see if he could see the back number plate of the car. It was also covered with another bag. This was confirmation that whoever had been driving the people carrier had purposely hidden their number plates. That automatically made them suspect number one. They had to find the car, find the driver and hopefully then they would find their offender. Carly's heart was beating fast and she had to steady herself as she shouted out to the team in the room with her.

"Get every single camera that car has passed and will pass on the screen" Carly instructed. We cannot afford to lose sight of it at all. Everyone in the room nodded in agreement and they set up the system to follow the car.

The time on the camera was showing 23 minutes past midnight. They were able to consistently follow the car as it continued to drive through the high street, where Billy had just walked and up Station road. There was a roundabout at the top of the road leading from a dual carriageway and at that time of night, despite a few other cars around, they still had no trouble following their car with its number plates hidden. The car drove the whole way around the roundabout and came back on itself, undeniably heading towards the river. At the next roundabout, predictably the car turned left as the route would naturally take it. The camera followed the car until it went round quite a sharp bend in the road. The next camera didn't show the car continuing it's journey.

"Fuck" exclaimed Carly. "How have we lost it?" she stared at the screen.

"It's ok," Daniel replied, "you know on that corner is the tiny car park used by the nursery and the football team. We can get the CCTV from the little club house there, I bet that's where it parked up".

One of the other offices in the room was immediately on the phone to the nursery, and they did have CCTV footage. The police were welcome to come down and collect it at any time. Daniel already had his car keys in his hand by the time his colleague hung up the phone.

"I'll be back as soon as I can," he said, skipping off down the corridor. The excitement in the station was heating up. Carly couldn't sit still and wait. She put a call in to see where her boss was, and left a message for him to call back. DI Sidhu called back a few minutes later to say he was on his way back to the station and to get the room ready for a team meeting. That included drinks and sandwiches, it was going to be a long afternoon.

James and Daniel both arrived back at the station within minutes of each other. Carly had been busy putting more notes up on the wall, and had come to the conclusion that Billy Ashton was not the most loved citizen in town, and potentially had ruffled the collar on a number of people across the area. She took notes off her boss and Daniel to add the wall as the rest of the team looked on whilst enjoying their free lunch.

James updated them all on his findings of the morning and instructed Carly to find Debbie Katz to speak to her and get an alibi if she had one. Carly went off to make the call whilst Daniel put the disc of the new CCTV footage from the nursery into the machine for them to watch.

It was perfect, the footage was a stable continuation of the street CCTV they had just left. The car was seen to park in the far corner of the nursery grounds. Almost hidden as it was parked so close to the bushes and trees, but it was there all the same. And finally, the driver got out of the car. A dark hooded long coat hid the appearance of the driver. Daniel sighed at the non-distinguishable character, but didn't take his focus from the screen. Billy got out the other side, he stumbled around to be with the hooded figure, who's gloved hand went around Billy's waist to stabilise him. The driver was slightly shorter than Billy himself and looked as if they were struggling to keep him upright.

"That has gotta be someone he knows." Daniel muttered. "He seems quite at ease, despite being pissed out of his mind. And look, they're taking him through the shrubs into the field. That's not an easy route to walk. It's all prickles and branches, but it saves walking all the way around the front via the road. We have to get back down there to look for fibres in the shrubs."

One of the other offices agreed to go down there immediately.

The camera showed the two figures struggling to push through the bushes, arms still around one another, but at one point Billy put his head up high to look more clearly at his associate and appeared to reach his hand down to his crotch, giving a little thrust before stumbling again, and holding tightly onto the arm of the other person.

The CCTV lost them as they went through the bush.

"Do you think that's a woman?" Daniel asked. "Billy looked like he was getting excited. Was he on a promise of something? But that definitely isn't Cat. She's quite a bit shorter than Billy, and this person is maybe only an inch or two. I can't see a pair of stilettos getting through that growth of trees and bushes, can you?" he asked generally to the room. He continued thinking out loud "I guess it doesn't have to be a woman. More reason for Billy to go off in secret, if he was having an affair with a man!"

Daniel turned to the white board, pen in hand and asked everyone in the room for their thoughts. At that moment, Carly came back into the room. She had managed to get hold of Debbie Katz who swore she was in Germany on Friday. She lived in a town called Munster and had only come back to the UK for a few days to see her parents in Surrey and meet Louise for lunch. They would have to verify her whereabouts and check with her neighbours and workmates in Munster. Debbie still lived alone, about a ten minute drive from her aunt, with whom she wasn't particularly close. She now worked, still in insurance but for a small company dealing in shipping. She admitted it was the opposite environment to that of the London office and she was happy that social gatherings were limited to a Christmas lunch and nothing else. She had sounded quite convincing but Carly knew better than to trust everything she was told. She took the pen off Daniel and added her own comments before continuing where he had left off.

Without missing a single word, she wrote down everything her colleagues were saying about the details found on the camera. Mum type car, indescribable long dark coloured coat with a hood, but with a slight indent giving the coat some shape around the waist area. Perhaps there was a belt on the coat, or belt hooks. The car number plates were definitely hidden, the driver certainly didn't want to be seen on foot at all. Billy was showing signs of drunken excitement. Was this a planned meeting or a surprise for him? He was definitely not being visibly or physically forced through the hedge. On closer look, the gloves that the perp was wearing appeared to have a leather shine to them and were really tucked up inside the sleeves of the coat. These weren't short woollen gloves.

Once the team had a long list of ideas, they went back to the camera and patiently waited for the driver to return.

It was a long wait, almost an hour until the figure walked in through the main entrance of the car park. They hadn't decided to walk back through the bushes to return. It was still impossible to see a face, the hood was firmly up in place. The footwear was also very dark in colour but Carly could just about see that their person was wearing Chelsea boots, a simple ankle boot with no laces. Again this was a unisex choice of footwear, but it didn't look like it was particularly large.

The phone call came back from the team who had gone down to the nursery. They had two sets of fibres from the bushes, two separate pieces of material. One was from the jacket that Cat had said Billy was wearing when he left the house, the other looked as if it came from a parka style coat. A little too heavy for most people to be wearing in the very mild May weather. They also had footprints. Of course there were loads of prints going to and from the entrance to the nursery building, but there were distinct prints right by the material they found. It was easy to identify two sets. One was the size 11's owned by Billy, the other pair were much smaller. Size 6. "Not ruling out any small footed men, but size 6?" Carly questioned. "If we need to rule out small footed men, let's do that, but I think I'm ready to concentrate on all the women in his life now." She continued. "From listening to the gossip at school, Cat wasn't the only woman. There were rumours he was having an affair. Was it just the one? Or was it just a one off? Was he murdered by a jilted lover? Was it Debbie from the office or one of the other many women he had seduced?" She stopped to think about what she had just said, whilst Daniel took over the writing on the board for her. "Was he being led into the field for sex?" she asked. "Was it a sex act gone wrong? Could it possibly not have been murder but a terrible accident?"

They went back to the CCTV footage of the character returning to their car. There was a lot of shoulder movement, as if the character was either crying heavily or shaking through fear. They were seen walking to the boot of the car this time, and a hand reached out to open the boot, the sleeve of the coat riding part way up the arm, but still the arm was covered by the long glove. The person took what looked like an empty bin liner from the boot, closed the door and returned to the front of the car. They were still keeping extremely well hidden from the cameras. Was that planned too?

There was noticeable movement in the car, was the driver getting changed? The body was moving a lot whilst remaining seated in the driver's seat. The gloved arms were waving around and for a moment it was visible that the coat sleeves had come off, although a hood of some sort stayed on the head. A short moment later, the car reversed back fully out towards the road. A quick glimpse of the front of the car showed no more clues to the driver, hood was still firmly covering most of the face, but this time Carly could just about make out a naked hand with nail varnish on it. "The gloves are off," she shouted out. "Look, you can see this person is wearing varnish, it's a very feminine looking hand." Everyone crowded around to look more closely. It was the right hand, so no wedding or similar rings were detectable, but there was definitely nail varnish and slender fingers.

The officers went back to following the driver on all the public CCTV they had available. The driver carried on driving towards Molville, but turned off down the lanes of Coes Green. There were still a considerable amount of CCTV cameras in that area, until the car turned off a side road that led to the much smaller villages surrounding Oldcoewood. Too many lanes without cameras meant that after 15 more minutes of following the car, they lost it. The officers who had attended the scene at the nursery followed the route and within half an hour had found two discarded carrier bags along one of the lanes that the driver may have driven down. The evidence was zipped up and shipped back to be analysed.

Carly was devastated that she couldn't follow her suspect all the way back home, but still delighted with the information they now had. This was a significant step up in the case, they had visibility of the last person to see Billy alive, and a good guess that it was also their murderer. Carly was going to concentrate on Billy's female followers, and would start by going back to school and looking at the feet size and height of the mothers collecting their children.

16.
CLAIRE

Claire had told Cat that she would pick the kids up after school and bring them back home. She wanted to do everything she could to help her friend, but more importantly, she wanted to be seen to be helping her friend and be seen to be the number one support. She also wanted to keep out of Wayne's way. He was working from home, and it felt like he was watching her every move. She was in no mood for afternoon delight and also not in the mood for her every twist and turn to be scrutinised. She didn't know why Wayne was watching her so closely, but she found it very unnerving. Of course she wouldn't say anything to him, she was a good and dutiful wife, her place was to support Wayne and provide for him. So naturally at lunch time she sat with him to eat lunch and made polite conversation about his work. It was a difficult time as the market for Conservatories was slow. They relied heavily on the commission Wayne would bring in to keep their lifestyle at a level with the likes of Jaycee and Simon.

Claire had grown up in a very strict home in South Wales with her Vicar father and housewife mother. She had been brought up to follow all the rules and her father certainly ruled the house with an iron fist. Claire had often seen her mother cowering in the corner of their large stone kitchen, whenever her father was angry, but then he would switch back so quickly into his Vicar mode to forgive her and she would get back to being the almost perfect housewife. Claire was an only child and had been quite spoiled by both her parents, but she had been a good child too. She would always help out around the house, because she knew that if her mother was happy then she would give her the freedom to go out into town with her friends whenever she wasn't at school, she would also always come home to a freshly cooked meal and always a nice pudding to match. When her father was happy with her, he would gift her little things; a trinket box, a pair of earrings. Claire learned very quickly to be a perfect young lady growing up and that gave her the freedom and the tools to do whatever she wanted. She was also extremely observant. She knew that when her father was in the Church, chatting to their parishioners and making everyone feel so much better about themselves, her mother was feeling so much better with Mr Jones, the local Butcher. Claire would laugh, as she saw herself living in a real life rural drama, where everyone knew what they thought was everyone else's business but everyone kept their own secrets behind closed doors. She wasn't sure if her mother knew that she knew about her affair with the Butcher. When she was bored, she would saunter into the kitchen to ask her mother what was for dinner. If it was a vegetarian option she would sigh loudly, and say to her mother "Don't you just fancy a big, fat juicy sausage from the Butcher Mum" as she skipped out of the room to giggle behind the door. The affair had been going on for years and years but she knew that her mother still loved her father, so it wasn't in Claire's interest to change anything. Life as it was, was good for Claire, but she made sure that she stored the information for times when she wanted to get something from her Mother.

Claire had tried her hardest to dig the dirt on her own father too, but he really was a very innocent Vicar. Very true to his congregation, his village and his family. She had pushed so hard at times to see if she could get a reaction out of him, or a clue that he wasn't the perfect Vicar, but she failed each time. The only times her father got angry was at home. Maybe he did know about Mr Jones, but he never said anything to her mother, he would just get angry about insignificant things; his post being opened by her mother, his dog collar not ironed the way he really liked it. Each time Claire's mother would apologise and mutter under her breath that she wouldn't do it again. They would smile at each other and get back to their happy home life.

Claire could see how her mother got the best out of both lives, and she liked what she saw. She soon realised that she could do the same, and as she grew up, went to college and then got her first secretarial job she took it upon herself to scrutinise and get inside the heads of everyone she came into contact with. If she liked them, then she would make them fall in love with her, make them realise that they needed her in their lives so that she would be at the forefront of their thoughts for every event and every occasion. If she didn't like them then she brought them even closer to her, so that when those who she didn't like fell in love with her, she could manipulate them to do whatever she wanted them to do until she was bored, then she would just walk off and leave them, pining after her, into the sunset.

Claire used her Marilyn Monroe hourglass figure to flirt continuously. It didn't matter if she was in a relationship when she was introduced to someone new. It didn't matter if they were male or female, gay or straight she would always saunter over with her ample breast lifted and poised in the right direction, so that her audience couldn't help but notice her. She always touched people when she spoke to them, and whispered so that they had to lean in closer to her to hear what she had to say, and when they leaned in, she leaned in even closer so that they could smell the light perfume, sprayed delicately into her cleavage. She wanted to be a sex symbol and in her late teenage years would rarely go home alone after a night out.

But when Claire met Wayne, she thought she would put an end to her flirting. He was the best looking guy she had ever set eyes on. He was in Cardiff on a work conference or something, and Claire had moved out of her village into the City centre.

They both happened to be in the same bar at the same time, having gone there straight from their respective offices. Naturally, Claire had been wearing a tight pencil skirt and a blouse unbuttoned a little too low for office attire, and a pair of killer heels that she had taught herself to wear and bear from a young age. Heels added so much to her overall look and gave her a little more height to position her bosom in the right place. Wayne had walked into the bar, untying his tie as he walked and laughing with a couple of colleagues. He went straight to the bar and ordered a round for all of those he had come in with. Claire watched with great interest. Here was an extremely good looking man, who was generous too. She knew she had to make herself known to him. Within half an hour, she had Wayne all to herself, fully focused on building a new relationship with her, and they had both left their work colleagues as they found a snug in the corner of the pub to get to know one another a little better. It was a no-brainer that she would eventually go back to his hotel room with him and that they would spend the rest of their lives together.

Claire put her flirting on hold whilst she devoted all her time to ensuring that Wayne would fall madly in love with her, and it worked. Within 6 months she had moved down to Oldcoewood to live with Wayne and had got herself a part time secretarial work in a local solicitors firm. They were married after a year and naturally had a huge wedding back in her home village, where they could invite everyone in the village, plus everyone Wayne had ever known to their huge celebration. She then set herself a new target to provide her new husband with everything he could wish for. She was an excellent cook, just like her mother and very loyal and understanding in the bedroom too. Naturally, her old habits did try to sneak back, but she did everything she could to stay loyal, and spent a lot more time at home cooking rather than risking going out and meeting new people. She knew that she had put on a bit of weight, but also recognised that just made her boobs even bigger and she wore appropriate clothing to enhance this whenever she could. She also knew that people still looked at her, and she reckoned that she still had the power to manipulate anyone she wanted to. It was in her blood.

But back at home now, sitting with Wayne at the kitchen table, trying to avoid his glances, Wayne asked Claire if she was going to the gym that day. She hadn't decided if she was going to. If she did it would just be for a gentle swim. She felt achy around her shoulders and didn't want to aggravate them anymore and do further damage. She nodded and told him she was going though, and set off an hour before school pick up. She had to get her car washed and give it a tidy up. She hated it being a mess and was convinced that the kids had left crumbs in it from the half term break.

And so she headed off to the petrol station car wash. It didn't do quite as good a job as the hand car washes in the area but it gave her some time to sort out the inside, whilst the rollers were sorting the outside. She was quite happy that it was actually very clean inside. She had done a good job with her hand vac earlier on. Whilst she sat in her car, the rollers beating around her, hiding her from the rest of the world, she contemplated her life. She really did love Wayne but she was now so, so bored. She needed excitement in her life again, she needed to be craved, and whilst she could demand the attention, the men that she knew locally, knew that she was off the market and politely left her to it. She wasn't as young as she was back in Cardiff, and needed to prove to herself that she was still in demand. She wanted to be wanted though and not just used because she was there. Her and Wayne had got into a system whereby she was on hand when it suited him, but he wasn't reciprocating like he used to. She wanted someone who would constantly look at her with eyes that said 'I want to take you, right here, right now', she wanted what Natalya had been getting from Billy and probably a dozen other men too. She had been loyal to Wayne for the best part of 14 years and now she was fed up. But she knew that Billy had had a specific thing for Natalya, and Natalya lapped up all the attention, her dresses had gotten shorter, her tops lower, her perfume stronger. She hadn't been doing that for her own husband, she had been doing it for the attention from other people's husbands. Claire wanted that too. That was her domain, and now Natalya was stepping on her toes. She had tried but failed and that made her angrier and more determined. Her low- cut tops made her chest look saggy and over tanning had given her wrinkles right up to her neck. She couldn't wear short skirts because she hated her thighs rubbing together, so would have to wear cycling shorts under them anyway. She did continue to flirt though and hadn't lost her touch there yet. She knew she was extremely good at it. Despite all that, the attention she was getting wasn't right. The men were looking at her boobs, but they weren't looking at her face. They weren't making eye contact with her, they weren't brushing past her, sidling up to her to make her heart skip a beat. They were just staring at her tits and talking about them to their mates, behind her back.

She had tried so hard with Billy. He was supposed to have been an easy target. Nearly always pissed and hands that wandered everywhere. Natalya had done it, so she should be able to too.

Cat was far too good for him, Claire thought, and she deserved so much better. It was time that Cat needed to know that her husband, correction, her deceased husband, had been a nasty, womanising two-timing rat, and because Claire hadn't been at the other end of his two-timing, it would have to be her to break the news to her friend. She needed proof though, and she was determined to get it from Natalya. A little blackmailing never really hurt did it?

Claire had a plan. She knew there was something up with Natalya, she had noticed that she hadn't moved at all when they were at Claire's the day before, and despite being the lazy one of the group, she literally didn't move a muscle whilst lounging back in Cat's sofa. She was keeping more than one secret, and Claire was going to find out what it was. What was she hiding? Was it more sinister than having an affair with her friend's husband. Could it be that she murdered Billy, could they pin the murder on her, or perhaps it was her smug husband Richard, who could do no wrong, always happy, pleasant, polite. What would he do though, if he knew his wife was having an affair? That wouldn't be any good for his street cred now. He wouldn't live that one down, and hold his head high amongst their group. It would crush him.

Without realising, the car wash had ended and the green light was flashing for Claire to drive out of the unit. She quickly put her mirror back into position, seatbelt on and drove out, still partly on auto pilot she found herself driving towards Natalya's house. She had over half an hour before school pick-up. maybe she could offer to pick Natalya's two up as well. The benefits of having a 7 seater people carrier was that she could fit loads of kids in her car. Pulling up outside Natalya's house, she could see that Richard's car wasn't there. She hoped he wasn't at home because she was going to make Natalya talk, admit to having an affair with Billy and she was going to record everything from her phone tucked neatly in the pocket of her jeans. She walked up the driveway and rang the doorbell.

Natalya answered the door and was very surprised to see Claire there. Despite being part of the same clique, she knew that she and Claire had never been as close as she was to some of the others. They were too similar in their ways and although they both hid it they both also knew it.

"To what do I owe this surprise?" Natalya asked Claire, trying to stand up as painlessly as she could, taking half a step back to hide partially behind the door.

"Oh I was just passing, but I thought you didn't look quite right yesterday, so I thought I'd pop in to see how are you, you know?" Claire replied.

"I'm ok, thanks" said Natalya, "just a bit under the weather. I think I've had a virus and it's knocked me for six" she was about to continue that she wasn't sure if it was contagious and maybe Claire shouldn't come in but Claire had already taken a step into the hallway, and she had no choice other than to open the door wider to let her in.

"Shall we put the kettle on then?" Claire suggested as she almost pushed past Natalya and walked into the kitchen. She had to take control of the situation and have the upper hand, otherwise she didn't think that Natalya would play ball. Both of them were dominant females who were used to taking full control of their situations.

She turned to get the cups out of the cupboard and only then noticed that Natalya was wearing what could only be a pair of surgical compression shorts. Claire recognised these from the multiple websites she had perused in her attempt to lose weight as quickly as possible. " Oh my god," she exclaimed. "You've had your legs done? Is it lipo? What else have you had done? You lied to us. You didn't tell us and we're all your friends" Claire was bursting inside with pride that she had discovered her secret so quickly, but also fuming that Natalya had the funds, probably in cash, to go in for the procedure.

"Not exactly lied" Natalya defended herself. "I just chose not to tell everyone. It's kinda private"

"Not between friends, it's not." Claire's respect for her friend had lessened a little. She was slim already anyway, so why was she having more work done? Was it purely for attention or to show off her additional wealth that Richard had made. "How much did that set you back? How much did they suck out?" Claire concluded that once again, it was Natalya who would be first out of them to try something different, and put her husband's money where her mouth was.

"Well, you know what it's like" Natalya was partly relieved that her secret was now not such a secret, but also pissed off that it was Claire who dragged the information out of her. "Not necessarily the sort of thing you would shout about. I didn't realise how much it would bloody hurt though. I'm so battered and bruised and it's agony to walk. I've spent the weekend trying to move as little as possible. It's a killer".

She had gone in for the liposuction procedure the week before but hadn't realised how painful it would be and the recovery time was taking a lot longer than she thought (she actually didn't think about recovery time at all and hadn't planned for it). She admitted that she hadn't told anyone although Cat had guessed when she was at her house at the weekend. All of this wasn't helping Claire to feel any better about herself, as her jealousy was getting the better of her. They moved into the lounge with their tea. Whilst they were adjusting the cushions to settle down, Claire checked her phone and subtly set it to record.

She brought up the subject of Billy quickly, as she knew she was short on time. She had never been late to pick up the children from school and was conscious that she was picking up Cat's too.

They spoke about how terrible the whole situation was, how terrible for poor Cat and how they couldn't believe it had actually happened. Then Claire dropped the bomb. "I know you had a fling with him" she threw into the conversation.

Natalya's face dropped and she hesitated before answering "What the hell are you talking about?" She tried to stay strong but her heart was beating twice as fast.

"Jaycee knows too. We saw you sneak off with him at her house" Claire was building on catching her off guard. "Have you been seeing him for a long time?" She wanted to throw her questions at Natalya to keep her talking.

Natalya was stumped, there was no point in denying it now. "It's not like that at all" Natalya responded too quickly to defend herself any further. "It was a stupid drunken mistake, that's all. a one off. Please don't say anything will you. There's no point in hurting Cat, it's not like anything more can come from it!"

But Claire wasn't satisfied with that answer. She wanted to, no, needed to get on tape that it was more than a drunken quickie. She pushed and pushed for information until finally Natalya gave in. as she sunk back in her chair, she told Claire that it had happened about half a dozen times over the past year. She had loved the attention she had gotten from Billy. Despite it being the type of attention reserved more for loutish lads in their twenties ogling the half-naked girls on holiday. It made her feel young again, like a teenager. She was really struggling with her 40's and wasn't enjoying parenting very much either. She loved her children dearly, but she didn't want to parent them, to take them to child-friendly places. She hated zoos, she despised going to the movies and was just grateful they had passed the soft-play stage of their lives. She just wanted to party, look amazing and get drunk. She didn't care if she didn't have food in the house to feed them. They could make themselves ham and cheese sandwiches and she'd reminded her 9 year old son,

Samuel never to put metal in the microwave. The kids weren't too fussed about after school clubs and classes and so she didn't waste her time taking them to any. They were allowed on their computers whenever they wanted and both had TV's in their rooms so they were constantly entertained. The only reason she had started to spend more on her daughter Jess's clothes was so that she could borrow them too, if the need arose.

By the time they had to leave to collect the children from school, and Claire had suitably forgotten that she was going to offer to collect Jess and Samuel too, Claire had enough evidence on her phone. She nipped to the loo to check that it had recorded and immediately downloaded the recording to her Gdrive. There was no way she was going to accidentally delete this beauty.

Natalya changed into a proper pair of jeans, struggling to pull them up over her sore thighs and they left the house together, with Natalya reminding her again, not to say anything. To do it for Cat. That she had learned her lesson and Cat needed the circle to stay strong at this time. They couldn't fall apart in their group, not when she was on her own now.

Claire hugged her tight muttering that she was her friend and friends didn't betray one another. She hid her broad smile as she kissed the top of her friends' head and they got into their cars to drive up to school.

"Fuck" Natalya swore out loud as soon as she got into her car. "Fuck, fuck, fuck. That stupid nosey bitch" She thought to herself, 'I will never admit to that ever again, I will deny it for the rest of my life. She has no other proof. She can't do or say anything to anyone.'

When they arrived at school, Claire winked at her before walking two steps ahead and finding one of the PTA mums to chat to.

17.

Carly was in uniform when she returned to the school in the afternoon. She no longer needed to be inconspicuous, and wearing her uniform gave her the control she needed to approach as many of the parents as she wanted to. She headed to the gaggle of year 6 mums and immediately recognised the majority of them from the Facebook pictures.

Claire saw the policewoman walking towards her and her heart dropped into her stomach. Of course she should have expected the police to be up at the school, they were naturally doing their job and investigating, but the shock of seeing her without any forewarning was still a little alarming.

"Ladies," Carly addressed the group with a soft smile. She would usually call them out individually as she saw fit, but to address five mums in one go would take her far too long. She knew she was on borrowed time, as it was only a couple of minutes before the children came swarming out of their classrooms and everyone would get lost in a sea of bright uniforms and backpacks. "I'm so sorry for the loss of your friend" She continued. "I know you were part of a close-knit group with Mr Ashton and his family, and I would like to ask you some routine questions at your earliest convenience please". It wasn't normal practice to address a group like that, but Carly wanted to throw her bold statement into the group so that she could immediately assess the reactions. Two of the mums, Jaycee and Marie looked very sympathetic, Marie expressing her shock and upset at the news. They both nodded immediately and muttered their acceptance. Claire Edwards and Natalya Smith however both looked fearful, averting eye contact with her, avoiding looking at their friends and both simultaneously correcting their posture to regain a little control and hope that their appearances hadn't given anything away. Of course, with Carly's eagle eye she had noticed both the women's change in demeanour immediately. She made a mental note to start with those two. The 5th woman, Tanya Brown nodded in sympathetic agreement with Jaycee and Marie.

"It's just unbelievable" Claire joined in with Marie's remarks, "devastating for our poor Cat. And those boys... without their father" She couldn't stop herself from taking the lead "How awful for them. Thankfully they have us all to help them out, and I will be taking the boys home to their poor mother this afternoon." Carly could sense this drama show unwinding. As a teenager, she had been involved with the local Am Dram society and as part of her police training had enhanced her personality testing skills, reading body language, noticing change in tone, volume and voice. She was proud of her ability to quickly understand her audience. It was such an important part of police work, to identify the storytellers amongst the others. This woman was certainly up for an Oscar with her acting skills. Her arms were positioned perfectly to enhance her voice and her tonal balance was spot on for someone having mastered the devastated friend speech. It may just be that she wants to be the centre of attention, Carly thought. Some people just couldn't cope with other's having their own performance and had to get involved, had to have their name up in lights, alongside the leading body.

Carly thought that Natalya Smith looked more terrified and stayed completely quiet. What did she have to hide? Carly turned to Natalya first. Claire would need to write her script, and Carly was amused at the thought of giving her time to present the most elaborate and carefully written scenario that she could. She would be ripping it apart at the seams as soon as Claire started presenting it, anyway. "Is there a chance you could come down to the station later this afternoon please?"

she asked. "Of course, if that is going to present a problem" she noted the tensed shoulders and wanted to stop a negative answer, "I'm more than happy to come to your house with my colleague but I don't know if that will worry your children" she added.

"I, um, I'm not very well" Natalya responded all the same. "I've had a virus and I'm still recovering. Can I come later in the week?"

Carly was not prepared to handle this on other people's time. "I'm sorry, Mrs Smith. That's not an option. As you can surely understand, we are dealing with a potential murder case." She looked Natalya directly in the eyes as she spoke, and watched them widen in fear as she voiced the word 'Murder'. "Shall we say five o'clock this evening then. That will give you time to get your children home and settled before you have to come out again."

Natalya was still fighting back though. "I really can't come out tonight," she argued. "My husband is at work, and the children have activities they need taking too. I can't leave them alone" she continued. Carly looked around the rest of the group at the mother's only too eager to help out if it meant that Carly could get her job done. She raised her eyebrows at Natalya and allowed her to finish speaking.

"Can you come over tomorrow morning instead?" she almost begged. Natalya knew that Richard had a company meeting the following day, she didn't want him around when she was speaking to the police. Naturally, he would expect her to be interviewed, but if she did it when he was out, there would be less chance he would question her about it afterwards. She wanted to keep her interview very private if she could. But she also reminded herself that she had nothing to hide, and nothing to confess to. She started to plan the interview in her head. It would be a short and courteous meeting to talk about her dear friend Cat, and her poor deceased husband. Nothing different to what the other women would be saying.

Carly agreed to visit Claire after going to see Natalya's the following morning. It would give her the rest of that Monday afternoon to link some more evidence together and talk to her boss about the women from Billy's workplace. It also meant that she could get PC Daniel Gold to accompany her too. Two pairs of eyes were always better than one, especially when in the interviewees house. He would happily, and in great detail, take down the notes so that she could concentrate on gauging her interviews and probing further afield into the lifestyles these people led. She took down all the phone numbers of the ladies in the group, promising to call the others following the first two interviews to arrange times for them as-well. She wasn't sure that she would actually need to interview the others for anything more than a confirmation of the facts that she already knew so well. Her eggs were all pretty much in a basket she was naming Claire and Natalya. She was expecting to get a lot more information from those two to help knit the case even closer, understand the real Billy Ashton and lead to nailing the Bastard that had ended his life.

As she had predicted, the playground suddenly filled with all the colours of the rainbow as the children ran out and dispersed themselves amongst the waiting adults. Claire waved over to the Year 6 and Year 4 teachers respectively and declared loudly that she was to take Ned and Jason home to their mother. She spent a little time talking to the two class teachers whilst the kids ran off to play. Carly noticed that neither Ned nor Jason seemed particularly despondent or reluctant to join in with their friends. Very strange that two boys who had just lost their father were not displaying any signs of grief. Maybe that was a good thing. The school, she knew from previous experience, had a very caring staff and they would have been briefed about how to deal with grief and mourning. She would have liked to see how the boys reacted when they returned home, but didn't feel that she could warrant turning up just to see that but would instead check in with her family liaison officer later that afternoon to see if Cat had arranged any time with her, although Cat had been reluctant to book that in, as she was determined, with her parents at home too that she could manage.

She would also speak to Cat again later and ask how the children were getting on. If she could persuade her to spend some time with the liaison officer, June, she was confident that June would report back in detail. As a trained child Psychologist, she could read between the lines, understand where the grief lay and distinguish between all the emotions.

Carly also wanted to have a quick chat with the teachers too and roamed over to where they were standing talking to Claire. As they saw her approach they both tried to end their conversation with Claire abruptly, to give their full attention to the advancing Police Officer.

Claire looked quite put out but held her head high as she turned to call the three children to her, making a point of putting an arm around both Ned and Jason as they walked off towards the car. Maybe Carly was being too harsh, but she also noticed the glance that the year 4 teacher gave Claire as she walked away. She followed the teachers up toward the main block and they headed into the staff room for some privacy.

Carly explained that she just wanted to know how the children had been at school, and if the teachers had overheard or witnessed anything of concern.

The report back from both the teachers was that the kids joined in almost as normal. They were both smart and studious children. Jason had had a moment when he wanted to leave the classroom, and the head teacher had taken him off to the library for a while. They had sat together, and she asked if he wanted to talk about his dad. He had replied that he didn't, but he was sad because he didn't feel like he wanted to talk to his friends about anything at all. He had been reassured that he didn't have to do anything, speak to anyone or explain anything that he didn't want to, and that comforted him enough to go back to his class. Ned had naturally also been quiet today but had a strong group of friends who sat glued to his side.

The staff reiterated that they were happy either way if the boys wanted to come to school or spend time at home with their mum. It was a difficult time, and they were having to review their own training in grief to best understand how to talk to the children. It looked as if they were doing a great job of it anyway, and Carly was happy to leave them to care for the children if they did decide to continue going into school.

When she left the school, Carly rushed back to the station to look at the brainstorming wall. She immediately put a question mark by Natalya Smith and Claire Edwards. She wanted to cross out Marie and Jaycee, especially as Jaycee was barely 5 foot tall and had tiny feet. They had determined that the perp had much bigger feet, but there was of course nothing to stop someone wearing shoes a few sizes too big. Of course, that may have impacted their ability to walk and climb through hedges, but she still didn't want to rule her out completely. Whilst she had been talking to the mother's in the playground, she had also noted their size and shapes. Marie was quite tall but had been away for the weekend, and had photographic evidence and a strong alibi from her husband Lee, who had already been in to talk to them. The photos from her weekend were already on Facebook to justify that too. She had been with her parents, it would just take a quick call to verify the truth in that. But there was no rush, Carly didn't think that she needed to spend much time on Marie in this first instance. Claire was the tallest of the group with quite large feet. Natalya was slightly shorter than Claire but also had quite large feet. Jen and Fiona hadn't been at pick-up so Carly was unable to assess them in person, but she knew from looking at the photos that their builds weren't a great match. Jen and Fiona were both larger in relation to their friends. Maybe not as athletic and their shapes would be more noticeable on camera.

Carly enjoyed matching the new information to that which she already had on the wall. Her focus was definitely Natalya and Claire, but she could also see that Debbie Katz had been added to the wall too. It wasn't an all-female list either, there were a couple of other names from Billy's work as well as his group of friends and then there would still be investigations into the other rugby dads and really anyone who had had a gripe with Billy. It wasn't a small list and would take a long time if they were to go through each person individually. Carly was convinced that her gut instinct would help her though and she wanted to sit down with her boss to fully understand what his thoughts were on what they had found out about Debbie too.

18.

As Claire was driving the children back to Cat's house, she was desperately trying to decide how to break the news of Natalya's affair. Should she tell Cat herself, and swear her to secrecy? But then if Cat knew, how could she pretend not to know when she next saw Natalya, amid all the emotions she was currently going through, she would naturally be so angry and disappointed, let down by one of her close friends. She might also be dubious of why Claire was the one telling her too, after all, Claire was great at keeping secrets. No, she decided she would have to let Cat find out for herself.

Perhaps she could leave the recording on a USB somewhere that Cat would find it? But then her own voice was on the recording and there would be no doubt that she would be recognised. She was frantically trying to think of how she could pass on her news, and still remain the blue eyed best friend who only had her friend's interests at heart. Then she had an idea. She was told about the affair from a third party, and was only going to do the right thing by her friend. She couldn't bear to know about it and not support Cat. But who did she hear the gossip from? By the time she reached Cat's house she had decided that she had overheard Ellen and Harriet talking about it in the playground. She hated Ellen anyway, so it wouldn't hurt to spread a little rumour about her too. She was a meddling nosy cow who couldn't just do what was asked of her by the PTA but had to question everything each time, and put her stupid opinion across. Claire and Ellen had fallen out a number of times, and the latest one had resulted in a slanging match in the middle of the street that ended with Claire having to apologise to Ellen. She would never forgive her for that. And as for Harriet, well she was no threat really to Claire, but her son and Claire's own son didn't really get on at school. Harriet's son Josh wasn't a Rugby player. He was an amazing artist, with a very dry sense of humour for an 11 year old, and his WhatsApp messages really wound her Ethan up. Ethan didn't quite understand that the comments Josh made were purely for entertainment, certainly not malicious or spiteful at all, but they made Ethan angry enough to hurl his phone across the room at times. Poor Ethan was quite highly strung and didn't like to be made a fool of. Yes, she decided that she would blame the gossip on them and be right by her friend's side to pick up the pieces and decide what they should do about Natalya. And then there would be the obvious question of whether to tell Richard or not. Claire was excited by the time she parked up in the driveway and switched off her engine.

Claire put on her best-friend face as she helped the boys out of the car and headed towards the front door. She was greeted by an extremely teary Cat. "You're obviously having a shit day today then" Claire said as jovially as she could, trying to lighten the moment.

"Oh God Claire '' Cat replied, "I've just sat in our room all day, looking at his stuff, trying to remember all the best memories in each of his outfits. To be honest, it's his England Rugby jumper that I remember the most. When we used to go to the games before the boys were born, and then we did go to a few of the games after the kids arrived into the world, but then he stopped taking me because I was cheaper than a babysitter, and the kids couldn't stay in the pubs til 11pm or whenever kicking out time was. And then I found his wedding suit. He was so handsome on our wedding day, and he smelt divine! Isn't that funny, I remember his smell really well then, but I don't really remember it from other times. I think it was because he didn't smell of beer during the ceremony" she laughed out loud "of course, he had had a couple, but not loads' ' she continued. "Just to take the edge off the nerves he told me when he kissed me at the altar. But I have been looking for things that I don't recognise too. I don't know why but I want to be angry with him again, like I was yesterday. I want to find fault and catch him out. I want to be so angry for him leaving me but also angry in other ways." Cat hesitated, not really knowing how to express her feelings and knowing that she was jabbering on without any structure.

"But you can be angry with him, and love him at the same time" Claire offered. "You know he was a bit of a shit at times, a bit disrespectful" she added.

"Yes but that was Billy. That defined him and I married that, whether it was the right thing to do or not. I knew what I was letting myself in for, I knew that he was far from perfect, and I was far from number one on his list, but I want, no, I need to be angry with him in a way that I wish him dead. That is so wrong isn't it? And for God sake don't tell that to the police woman or she'll have me banged up behind bars."

"Oh God Cat" Claire closed the door to the kitchen where they had moved to, so the children or Cat's parents wouldn't hear. " I might have that information for you!"

"What are you talking about?" Cat was suddenly unsure if she really did want to hear of things that would have made her wish her husband dead.

"Well, I can't say if it's completely true, because I heard it from Ellen and Harriet, and you know what a mixer that Ellen is. But I heard that your Billy was having an affair. Not just a fling or a one night stand. An affair with someone close to us" she added the last sentence for effect, turning to face Cat straight on and with eyes that said 'I am your support and I am your shoulder to cry on'. Cat looked back at Claire but without the immense shocked expression that Claire was expecting. "Go on" she calmly encouraged instead.

"Well," Claire started to feel nervous. Was she doing the right thing? What would she get out of this? She hadn't actually blackmailed Natalya. She had just recorded her confession to pass on to her friend. "I'm not exactly sure how much evidence there is, and if it's definitely that person" she backtracked. "I just heard them saying they had heard someone mentioning him in line with her."

"Mentioning him how? Who mentioned him? What the hell did you hear Claire?" Cat was starting to get angry. Claire had dug her hole too deep and couldn't get out of it now. She had to just come out with it, or she would look really stupid, and that certainly wasn't her plan. "They said they knew that Natalya was sleeping with him. Apparently she has been for a while." The relief to get it out of her system was all too much and Claire felt herself welling up. This was it, this was her putting herself in pole position within their friend group, mother hen (although she hated that phrase) and the one holding the keys to all the secrets.

"I know that!" Cat said bluntly.

"What?" Now it was Claire's turn to be shocked. All her emotions suddenly disappeared "How do you know? Why have you not told me this?" If Cat knew that her husband had been having an affair with Natalya, why was she still friends with her? Why had she not told the rest of the group?

"Because I wanted to stay married, I liked my life as it was, despite all the shit I've put up with for years. My friends and our group mean more to me than anything. What would I do if I split the group up by confronting Nat? Where would that have left me? More alone than ever, with a husband who would hate me more than he's ever hated me and a group of best friends who would have to split their loyalty to two sides. We all know that's impossible to do. I've hated Billy for that and Nat too for ages. I'm an idiot I know, a stupid pathetic idiot but it is what it is. I'm not saying anything to Natalya now that Billy is dead. As far as I'm concerned it's all over, done with."

Claire was speechless. She had planned to be the shoulder to cry on, to put their so-called cheating friend right in the shit, maybe even suggest that she is a prime candidate to be a suspect to Billy's murder. But Cat's admission to knowing this all had stopped her dead in her tracks. Where did she stand now? She couldn't think of anything to say that would get her out of the very large hole she had just dug. "I'm sorry." Was all she could think of saying.

She left soon after that, muttering about having to put the boys' dinner on before their cubs' and scouts' groups that evening.

As Cat closed the door on her, she slumped down onto the floor and wept. Her mother came out of the lounge and sat down with her on the hard wooden floor of the hallway. "Mum" she said through her tears, "Mum, my life is completely fucked. My husband is dead but he was a horrible bastard to me throughout our marriage. I don't know what I'm supposed to think and I don't know what I'm supposed to do."

"There is no supposed to," her mother replied, "you do whatever the hell you like. If you want to book yourself a holiday to Ibiza for a week and sit by a beach drinking cocktails, then you do that. If you want the biggest funeral ever held and call the local paper to report it, you do that. If you don't want to do anything, you don't do anything. It's time for Catherine to come back, to break out of the mould she has been locked in and be herself. I'm so very sorry you've been through this, I'm sorry he wasn't a good husband to you. I'm sorry I didn't step in and put a stop to it all. But now is the time to put that behind you and start afresh."

"Thanks Mum," Cat said, burying her head into the comfort of her mother's hold. She sobbed until there were no more tears and then she started to think. It didn't take long before she had made her first decision. That she wasn't going to protect anyone apart from herself and her children. She called PC Cook to update her with the information she had been keeping a secret to protect her cheating husband and deceitful friend.

19.

As soon as Cat called Carly Cook with the update, Carly picked up Daniel in the car and sped over to her house. They spent another good two hours with Cat whilst she told them all about Billy's affair with Natalya, and how Claire had come round to try and break the age old news to her. Cat knew that Claire was trying to win her over, to get one upmanship over her friend and was disappointed when Cat had told her that she already knew the news. Carly and Daniel listened intently before providing their update on information. Carly told her that they had followed a people carrier to the nursery building, by the football pitch and had seen Billy with someone else squeezing through the hedgerow towards the river. It was still early days but they had clues they were following up, and they were confident they would find the killer sooner rather than later. "We aren't in a position of course just yet to tell you exactly what we have seen" Carly added, "but we would be grateful for any further information you can provide us about your friends' cars please."

Cat was comfortable to offer all the information Carly and Daniel needed regarding the cars that her friends drove. It was easy to identify the cars by which mothers were able to offer the most children lifts to and from their activities and parties. Of course the cars were family cars, and not just assigned to the women in the houses, although chance was the men kept to their smaller, sportier vehicles for showing off purposes and the excuse that they didn't have to chauffeur the kids around. Four of them had people carriers. Claire, Fiona, Natalya and Jen. This was great for the police to work on and helped them to reorganise their priority list yet further. They could move on to dissecting these four friends in greater detail, before moving out to the wider community of Oldcoewood and the surrounding area should they need to. "This is great, thank you Cat," Daniel said. "I can also tell you a little about Billy's work colleagues. We are investigating a few there, one who has moved to Germany but was back in the country quite recently. We've interviewed his boss and the PA. I think we're making good progress. Your help is so vital to this and we're very grateful" he concluded.

The information about his work was all new to Cat, she explained that she had never been involved with his work, never met any of his colleagues and had never even seen Billy's work phone, which was now in the hands of their DCI to look into his messages and calls.

Once glance over at Carly, and Daniel omitted to tell Cat the further details of Billy's active social life, involving a high number of other women. It was unnecessary at that time and would only cause more upset to the already grieving widow.

Once back at the station, Carly, Daniel and James huddled together to update the board. They could add a lot more factual detail about the names they had on the wall and match them to the figure in the CCTV. Jaycee was short, about 5 foot tall, and probably only a size 3 foot, so was moved down to the bottom of the priority list. Jen was quite tall and Fiona too, both were taller than Claire and stood shoulder to shoulder with a number of the men. But Fiona was all-round considerably larger than her friends. They couldn't see how she could fit the profile, or indeed fit through the narrow hedgerow for that matter. Thus she was relegated down beside Jaycee in order of significance.

James had updated the board with information on Debbie, after chasing up whether she had indeed returned to Munster when she said she had. There were discrepancies as she had told Carly that she took the ferry, as she liked to use different modes of transport to enhance her travel experience. They couldn't see where she had booked her ferry ticket, and still had no evidence that she was in Germany on Friday night. They agreed that they needed more proof of the visit, and would need to speak to Debbie and her parents again to request proof of travel, any hire car invoices and everything else that concluded her visit to her parents in the UK.

Carly and Daniel, having gone through all the information they had on the wall, had some concise notes to take them forward the next morning. They had prepared their interview questions for Natalya and were prepped to get going on that. Another long day, and they decided they had done all they could for now. Daniel had his family to get home to and Carly had promised Frenchie a long evening walk.

20.

Natalya was very nervous when she welcomed the two officers into her home on that Tuesday morning. They both accepted the tea that was offered and spent the time whilst the kettle was boiling to have a good look at their surroundings and their host. It was more than obvious that she was on edge. She was flushed and couldn't look either of them in the eye at any point of their conversations. She was visibly shaking when she handed the mugs over and sat herself down as far away from the two police officers as she could.

Once they sat down they started the questioning by asking her about her relationship with Cat. Natalya was happy to tell them how they were very close friends, she also had two children who were in the same classes at school with Ned and Jason. They spent quite a lot of their spare time together. "I have always been there for my friend Cat", Natalya said, trying to relax more into her seat as she was taking control of the conversation. "I was always a shoulder for her to cry on when Billy didn't come home and times, or really any time she was upset over one thing or another. She is quite an emotional person. Normally I mean, not just in this current awful situation!" She talked about the other women in their group, how they were all quite close and how they would go on holiday together each year to get away from the kids and the men for a week of sun and sangria. "Our holidays are amazing," she boasted. "A week of lying in the sun, not a care in the world, no men around, plenty of booze and sun-cream. That's all we really need" she smiled.

She was brought back down to reality with a bump. "Did Cat ever stray away from Billy?" Carly asked. "Do you know if she was seeing someone else behind his back?" She pretty much knew the answer to this already but wanted to change the direction of the conversation.

"No, I'm sure she wasn't and hasn't" Natalya replied quite confidently. "She was a very good wife to Billy. When we went on holiday, she didn't really look at anyone else. She wasn't really the flirty sort and often was too drunk to notice anyone else looking at her." Natalya seemed comfortable with her answers.

"And what about you?" Daniel asked. "Have you ever cheated on your husband, Richard?"

"What the hell has that got to do with Billy being killed?" Natalya snapped back at him. "But anyway no, I've never cheated on Richard. I'm very happily married, thank you" she said angrily. Her face reddening again.

"So you never had an affair or even a one night stand, a stolen kiss with Billy?" Carly butted in.

"Not at all" Natalya was very quick to answer but kept her head down as she blurted out her response. "How dare you assume that I had an affair." She raised her head to look at the officers, the first time she had made eye contact fully since their arrival. Her cheeks burned an even deeper red colour but she held herself high and maintained her contact.

"We weren't assuming," Carly responded calmly. "We were just asking the question".

"Well I haven't" Natalya replied bluntly. "Look, I don't have anything else I can tell you, so maybe we can wrap this up now please. I have a lot of work to do today."

Carly and Daniel stood to leave. "Oh, before we go" Carly turned to Natalya, who had already opened the front door for them to leave, "Do you mind if we have a quick look at your car?"

"My car?" Natalya asked. "Why would you want to do that?" she genuinely looked confused. "I suppose you can. Wait, I'll grab the keys." Carly and Daniel looked at each other. Natalya wasn't the driver of the car. She had no idea that Billy was picked up after he'd been to the pub. Unless of course it wasn't her own car she was driving. But then why would she swap her own car for one looking so similar. Her car was red, slightly muddy and there was a child's car booster seat placed in the front passenger seat. Of course, that could have been put there at any time, but the confusion when asked, and the willingness to immediately show her car to the officers, in comparison to her reluctance to open up about her own life and the obvious affair she was hiding, all said that this was definitely not the vehicle used.

They thanked Natalya and drove straight round to Claire's house, as Carly had arranged to do the previous afternoon. When they arrived, there was no one home. Daniel waited patiently at the front door after ringing the bell, whilst Carly took a walk around the property, as far as she could get to without climbing the gate into the back garden but they couldn't see any movement. There was no car parked out the front of the house either and no garage where it could be stored. Carly looked at Daniel. "For someone who has been so obliging and forthcoming with information on the others, and the eagerness to get all the info from us, does this seem a bit odd to you Daniel?" He nodded in agreement.

"I think we need to go and find the lovely Mrs Edwards."

Meanwhile, whilst they were on the hunt for Mrs Edwards, James Sidhu had contacted Debbie Katz's parents. They told him that whilst she was in England, she borrowed her mother's car.

A white Ford Galaxy 7 seater. They had that car because Mrs Katz senior was a childminder, and needed to ferry numerous children around at all times. They were convinced though that Debbie had taken the ferry back on her homeward journey to Germany on the previous Thursday, as she called to say she was back on French soil. That meant nothing though, and now with the knowledge that the car was also a people carrier, it put Debbie higher up the list. James called the Ferry company and requested their CCTV from the supposed boat that she had taken. It would take a little while to come back though, and in the meantime, he called back Debbie's mother to ask her to email over any recent pictures, facebook addresses or more. She was most obliging, convinced that her daughter was an innocent party, but didn't have any knowledge of social media accounts as she said "it is all too modern and technological to me, but I'm sure she doesn't upload any pictures anywhere".

On calling Debbie again to establish her social media standing, Debbie confirmed that after her experience with Billy, she came off all social media, preferring to keep her life as simple and hidden as possible. Her mother was able to email some photos though and they came through within a short while. Debbie was very attractive, with short spiky red hair. She looked to be of average height but also looked like she worked out a lot. There were photos of Debbie in sports clothes, and her muscles were quite visible, bulging arms showing through her lycra T-shirt.

Questioning her over the phone was difficult. Debbie was reluctant to offer information, citing her getting away from the past and putting it well and truly behind her, but eventually uncovered that she spent all her spare time in the gym, building on her strength in order to protect herself. She was never going to be put into a position where she felt undermined again. Her personal trainer had begged her to enter some body building competitions, but she had refused. It wasn't about showing off, it was about staying on top. She was definitely of a nervous disposition and despite her declaration, she obviously still thought about it a lot. Had her fear of Billy led her to come back to the UK to kill him?

21.

Claire hadn't gone home after dropping the boys off at school. She hadn't slept at all the night before, thinking about her conversations with Natalya and Cat. How had Cat known about Natalya and Billy and not told her? Did Natalya know that Cat knew? She couldn't have because she would have acted so differently towards Claire if it wasn't a secret. But then if Cat knew did Richard know too? She had to find out. Claire was fuming. She didn't like to be in the dark. As out and out leader in their friendship group, and it was her role to know what everyone was up to, even if she held her own cards so close to her chest. She decided that had to go and find Richard and see what he knew. When she drove up the road towards Richard and Natalya's house, she saw the police car parked outside. Natalya would have made sure Richard was out and had gone to the office if she was being interviewed by the police. Claire knew where Richard worked. He had recently refurbished a large office in Benton town and had invited them all to the grand opening when it had completed. He boasted how his office was for both work and pleasure, it had two beer fridges in and was a great escape for him and his business partner, Kevin to stay late in the evening. They had turned a meeting room into a games room, with a TV, games console and everything so that after they had finished work for the day, and the rest of the team had gone home, they could sit back, relax and not worry about rushing home to their other halves.

Completely forgetting that she had an appointment with the police officers, once they had finished with Natalya, Claire drove straight to Benton town. The traffic had calmed after rush hour and it took her just 10 minutes to get there. She found the office block in question and sat waiting for any sign of life to emerge. There was no one there, no cars parked outside, no signs of people coming or going through the glass doors. For a recruitment company, it operated in a strange way. She assumed that recruitment consultants were meant to be tied to their desks from 8am until 6pm every day. Maybe they were, and maybe the locals could take other forms of transport to the office, but if Richard had been there, his car would have definitely taken pride of place outside the front of the building . She decided to wait a while, to give herself some time to think about her next move, and it gave her the opportunity to spend some more time checking her car for rubbish and dirt. She was quite content that her car was spotlessly clean as she had stopped off the village en-route to Benton, to put a black sack she had filled up, into a public bin by a park. This bin had been almost full, and had a good scattering of the weekends' crap still lying around it. Disgraceful for a Tuesday that the council hadn't been round to empty the bins. Broken bottles, fast food boxes and much more were scattered around the green plastic. She wanted to make sure that her bag went into the bin itself, and had to remove some of the other rubbish to give her room. She was convinced that the council would be out to clear it sooner rather than later, otherwise the neighbours would be complaining.

After an hour of sitting just outside the office block, as discreetly as she could, she decided that Richard wasn't going to turn up at his office after all and she turned back towards Oldcoewood. She was thinking about Natalya and how she had completely gotten away with having an affair with their friends' husband, that smug look on her plastic face. How she thought she was so perfect. The sexy one of the group, the one who wore her daughter's clothes and dressed like a slut half the time. Claire hated her for being that person, for taking away the attention from herself, for having had a relationship with Billy. Claire's mind was on autopilot as she drove back and within ten minutes found herself outside Natalya and Richard's house. The police had left , she still didn't remember that they would have gone to her own house. She was so preoccupied with her emotions. And so she walked up to the front door and knocked. Natalya answered within seconds, looking flustered.

"Oh Hi Claire" she said, slightly relieved that it wasn't the police back again for more interrogation. Claire almost pushed past her to get into the house. "Are you ok?"

Claire still hadn't decided what she was going to do or say to Natalya but she knew she had to do something to give herself the upper hand, let everyone know who was at the top of this tree. "Does Dicky know you fucked Billy?" She blurted out as soon as the front door was closed.

"What the hell?" Natalya took a step back. "No he doesn't, and he won't ever have to. Please, what do you want, Claire?"

"What if he did know?. What if Cat accidentally found out?" Claire took a step towards her so-called friend. "What would you do to prevent that from happening?"

"Please?" Natalya started to cry. "What are you doing Claire? What the fuck do you want? Why are you doing this? We talked about it already. I fucked up, I know, but why do you want to keep going on about it?"

"Because you don't have your cake and eat it, you slutty bitch. You don't get to have surgery to change your shape and then take the pick of whoever you want, you whore." Claire was letting all her emotions out and feeling a lot better for it.

"But it wasn't like that" Natalya pleaded, "It was..." she didn't know what to say. It had been exactly as Claire was describing it. She had wanted more attention than she had been getting from her own, busy and aloof husband, and wanted to prove the work she had done would get her the notice she desparately craved. She had devoted her life to looking the best and getting all the attention.

"Have you ever done anything with Wayne?" Claire barked at her.

"Never" Natalya shouted back. "I've never touched your stupid husband. What has he got to offer me? He's just a pissed salesman who tries so pathetically to grab boobs and arses as he walks past. He's a creep and there's no way that his attention would make anyone else feel good about themselves. Billy made me feel so sexy, so young and so excited" she continued.

That was true, Claire thought. Wayne was a bit of a letch. He didn't hide his glares at the other women, but then again his openness surely made him more transparent if he was playing the field. Didn't it? Claire was still quite sure that her own husband hadn't had an affair, he couldn't keep a secret and she spent so much of her time checking up on him too. She focused back on Natalya. What *did* she want from Natalya, why had she turned up to interrogate her? What Claire really wanted was for Natalya to be hated by others, and not just herself, and she knew that Cat was too weak to end the friendship and tell the others. What would Richard do if he knew? Would he leave her or would he be as pathetic as Cat and accept it? After all, it wasn't as if the affair could continue, half of the party were dead! How could she win this battle and come out on top?

Natalya had noticed that Claire had slowed down, she wasn't jumping down her throat any more, and her initial aggression had calmed down a lot, Natalya realised that she hadn't prepared for this at all. Claire didn't know how to blackmail her. It was time to take back control of the situation before Claire came up with something else.

"Richard would never believe it if someone told him I was having an affair. I'm a wonderful wife to him. He knows how much I love him. Yes he knows I'm a flirt, but he's the man that I climb into bed with every night, my naked body winding around his, my lips on his and my hands all over him. He certainly wouldn't believe you, Claire. He would think you are mad. He doesn't like you very much anyway," She could see that she was starting to hit on a nerve, "he says you're annoying. You're always sticking your fat nose into other people's business. You should learn to step back and realise that no one cares for your opinion anyway.".

Claire was struggling. She could see that Natalya wasn't frightened any more and was fighting back. She knew she should have prepared this better but had acted on impulse. She was losing control and she hated this feeling more than anything. Unless she was in full control, Claire liked everything to be even and fair. If she gave something to one of her boys, she would immediately give the same to the other. She made sure that all the house parties took place in each house, and no one had the monopoly of hosting. If Wayne decided to treat her to a surprise, whether in the bedroom or a gift, she would naturally repay the favour and provide one back. That's how life worked. That's how everyone could always get along. But this wasn't happening.

If she hit out at Natalya then everyone would hate her. Instead, she had to defend herself from an attack by Natalya and become the victim. She wanted Natalya to lash out at her, but instead of riling her into a rage, she was somehow having the opposite effect. She was the one boiling under the skin, and Natalya had calmed right down and was now sitting on the couch waiting patiently for the next move.

Claire walked towards the kitchen.

"What the hell do you think you're doing?" Natalya called after her. "I think it's time you got out of my house, don't make yourself comfortable." She slowly followed her into the kitchen, not wanting to show any signs of the pain she was still experiencing from her procedure, and watched as Claire walked over to the block of knives by the stove.

"What…. No…. Don't be stupid" Now the panic set in, as she watched Claire reach for a knife. She stepped back into the hall where her phone was on the console table, and quietly picked it up.

Claire turned around to face her but instead of walking towards Natalya with the knife, she was holding it pointed towards her own face. "I'm not going to stab you, you fool." She said, "You're the evil one here Natalya. You are the one who is attacking me with your own knife. Your prints are already on here, mine are also on it now as I defend myself against you and try to survive your moment of madness, now that I have uncovered your deep, dark secret."

"You really have gone mad." Natalya whispered. "Put the knife down please Claire. We can sort this. No one will need to know anything. You're my friend. We've been friends for years. Why would we throw that away now? What is there to be gained from all this? Please Claire" she begged.

"You're not my friend." Claire answered back calmly. "You pushed your way into my group of friends. You turned up here when we were all perfectly settled and you pushed your stupid way in, tried to be top dog. Flirted with all our husbands, blamed it on the booze when you knew all along you had to prove you could shit on all of us, use us to make you look better. I know your type Natalya. I've seen it so many times before, and I don't like what you've been doing to us over the years"

"I really don't know what you're talking about Claire. Please just put the knife down and leave." Natalya gasped as Claire took another step towards her and pushed the tip of the knife into her own cheek, she pierced the skin just a tiny bit and a small drop of blood formed on her face.

"Oh Nat, that really hurt. Please don't stab me" Claire sarcastically mocked as she pushed the knife a little deeper. It was really hurting but she had to continue until the cut was deep enough to make an impact.

"Claire" Natalya yelled at her.

Just at that moment the doorbell rang. Both women stiffened. "Don't answer it" Claire glared at her. But Natalya was already halfway down the hallway "Just a moment" she yelled out towards the closed door.

Claire quickly put the knife down on the side, she now had a few drops of blood, very slowly dripping down her cheek, but nothing that a dab from a tissue wouldn't put a stop to. Natalya turned quickly and opened the door. The two police officers were standing at the door. Claire gasped and wiped at her face with the back of her hand. Shit, she had meant to meet them at her own house, now she would look suspicious. She had to think fast.

"Oh hello" she boldly thrust herself forward, a fake smile appearing on her face. She was even brash enough to put an arm around Natalya's shoulder as she reached the door.

"Why are you back?" Natalya asked the two officers.

"Mrs Edwards?" Carly asked, looking straight at Claire. "We called round to your house this morning as you surely can't have forgotten that we agreed to meet, but unfortunately you weren't there. As part of our investigation into the death of

Billy Ashton, we'd like you therefore to kindly come down to the station with us now to answer a couple of questions please."

"Oh I'm terribly busy at the moment, aren't I Nat?" Claire turned to Natalya. "I'll definitely be in tomorrow though, if you want to pop by for a cuppa then." She beamed with a big welcoming, Women's Institute kind of smile.

"I'm afraid this isn't a social chat, Mrs Edwards. If you don't come down to the station with us now, I will have to bring you in under caution."

Natalya stepped aside from Claire. "I think you'd best go off with them, Claire, go and answer the questions the police have for you." she said sternly. "Goodbye my dear." A huge grin crossed her face as Claire reluctantly picked up her handbag and followed the two officers out of the house.

She closed the door behind them and watched out of the window as they gently helped Claire get into the back of the squad car, her arms waving towards her own car parked on Natalya's driveway. She was obviously upset that she was being taken in and couldn't be trusted to drive herself there. Natalya watched as Claire continued to talk at the two officers trying to stay on top of the situation. It was worth the inconvenience of her car blocking part of her driveway just to see Claire being put into the back of a marked cop car. She glanced over the road and was even more pleased to see one of her neighbours peering out of her own window at the spectacle in front of her. Natalya caught her eye through the glass and waved. There would be no confusion that it wasn't herself being taken away.

22.

Whilst Carly Cook was talking to the two women at the door of Natalya Smith's house, Daniel Gold had been examining the second car that was on the driveway next to Natalya's own car, which they had previously examined. Assuming it belonged to Claire Edwards, this one was a grey Ford people carrier. It was spotlessly clean, having obviously been washed and cleaned inside and out within the past day or two. The wheels were glistening and looking through the window, the seats had been hoovered and there was not a crumb on the floor, despite the child's booster car seat in the back. It looked far too clean for Daniel. Had there been a conscious effort to have the car cleaned the day that the children went back to school after a week off, or was it for another reason? The car was also an excellent match for the car on the CCTV footage they had, he was more than sure of it. Daniel took photos from every possible angle, careful not to leave any detail out at all, and sent them straight back to the station for confirmation. It wasn't long before he got a response back to say that it definitely was a good fit for the car on the camera. They wanted to take it back to the station to give it a once over with a fine tooth comb. Daniel explained to Claire that her car would be brought to her for collection when she was finished at the station, but it was necessary for her to come in the police car as she had evaded their planned meeting. He would get a warrant to search her car fully, and it would be easier if they could do it onsite at the station rather than in her friend's driveway. He would also tell her this once she was safely in the interview room. Claire argued that she hadn't evaded them but had been worried about her friend, hence she had not been at home. That didn't wash with the two police officers at all and as Carly and Daniel drove away with Claire in the back of their car, Daniel waved to his colleague who was driving up the road towards the house to secure Claire's car and arrange for it to be removed.

He was pleased. He'd had a hunch about Claire Edwards when he had first met her. There was something too clean, too concerning and too untrustworthy about her. Now was the time for them to ascertain exactly what that was.

They drove back to the station calling in ahead to make sure their Chief Inspector was there and able to get ready for the interview. Carly wasn't going to waste a second more on their suspect, who, through her actions had moved to the top of the priority list. She didn't want to be toing and froing with this particular one. Once they arrived at the station, Carly had tried to make Claire as comfortable as possible, to relax her into opening up, but she was in a state. She had spilled her tea all over the table and her lap, she had almost fallen off her chair when she perched so precariously close to the edge of it. She was sweating profusely, and her hands were shaking.

When everyone was seated in the interview room, she began. "Tell me about last Friday" Carly started. She didn't want to start the conversation with closed questioning. She had enough time to listen to everything Claire had to tell her and wanted to see what was going to be offered before she took back the lead.

"We took the boys to the park by the lake for lunch," she said, trying hard to keep her voice steady. "Then we came home and they went on their games in their rooms. I think I put the washing away and watched a bit of TV. Don't ask me what I watched though, it was all a load of crap. We had Chinese for dinner, takeaway from KBR. Do you want their phone number to check? Because I have it here on my phone and you can see that I called them on Friday at about 6pm." She responded quite sarcastically, pleased that she had the proof on her phone.

"Thank you, we may look at that later." Carly responded with a smile. Claire wasn't expecting an affirmative answer to her question, it had been more of a rhetorical one. She didn't want them looking at her phone, she wanted them to accept her alibi and leave her the hell alone.

"What happened after dinner?" Carly prompted her.

"Got drunk on two bottles of wine." Was the blunt reply.

"And then what?" Carly realised the free flowing offer of information had come to an end. This is where she wanted the story to begin. It was of absolutely no interest to them what had happened up until the point when Billy left the pub.

"Fell asleep on the couch, probably woke up about midnight and went to bed"

Carly left that part of the conversation to one side, not convinced with the answers she was given, but was saving it for later. She changed the direction of the conversation to ask Claire about her relationship with Billy. The response again was blunt, no overt presentation of more information than was necessary. Claire stuck to the basics; he was her friend's husband and they saw each other at social events, her husband was friends with him, they both coached at the Rugby club. That was about it.

But Carly noticed that the eye contact wasn't there, unlike when Claire had talked about her takeaway Chinese. She wanted to probe further but had to be very careful how she worded her questions to get the most out of the answer, whether that would be verbal or facial expression. She glanced over at her Chief Inspector to check that he was happy with the way in which the interview was going. He gave her an affirmative nod as he sat back in his chair to observe the whole drama unfolding.

"Was Billy faithful to Cat?" she decided on keeping it impersonal, to take the pressure away from Claire for a moment. But testing Claire's knowledge of her friend's personal life.

"No" she answered promptly. She was happy with that question, it was obvious to her interviewers. And once again her communication flowed like the water running down a stream. "He was a two-timing rat. And Cat knew it. I'm surprised she put up with it actually, she was very weak around him, you know. But then she could have bottled everything up for so long and suddenly exploded. You never know with Cat, she was always quite calm on the outside, but you know what they say, you never know what goes on behind closed doors. I know if it were my husband, I'd kill him though, he would never get away with an affair. Oh, bad choice of words. Sorry!" A very small and subtle smile appeared for just a second. Carly didn't miss it. She knew that Claire had very carefully chosen her words and wasn't sorry to have mentioned Cat and kill in the same sentence. She was trying to build a picture in their minds, but their minds were far from thinking about Cat. Carly hadn't fallen for her words, she was just encouraged further to see what else she could get from the woman.

Carly nodded, made notes and continued with her next feeder line, all part of her exceptional planning, in the hope of guessing correctly what the answer would be before Claire actually spoke any words. She could see that Claire was ready to betray the whole group of friends, she was prepared to do anything to put herself in a better light. For Carly this was like taking candy from a baby. "And how did you know that he was cheating on his wife?" she continued.

"Because one of his mistresses was our friend Natalya" the answers were coming extremely fast now, as if there wasn't enough time to get all the information out. "She thought we didn't know but we did. She's been playing to him for years, wearing virtually nothing when we go out together, flirting and touching him far too much. It was so obvious, you can ask literally anyone."

"One of them?" Carly ignored everything she said about Natalya and focussed on the information she didn't already have. "How many did he have? Do you know?"

"No idea, but the bastard couldn't keep his dick in his pants. Sorry for the crudeness" slowly Claire's demeanour had changed again. There was no smile this time, but instead she spat her words out in anger. A small line of sweat started to appear on her brow.

"Have you ever had sex with Billy?" Carly was abrupt with her next question. "Were you one of them?"

"No" Claire looked down into her damp lap, where the tea had now left an unsightly stain.

"Have you ever done anything compromising with Billy? Anything that might be deemed as sexual activity but perhaps without the sex" Carly pushed. "I'm sure you know what I mean, without me having to spell it out!"

It was now that Claire hesitated before answering. "No" Still no eye contact. She started to outline the tea stain with her finger. Hopefully that would wash out of her skirt, she thought before focussing back to the questions being asked. "Why would you ask that when I'm so happily married?" She slowly raised her head to look back at Carly. "I've already told you that Wayne and I have a solid relationship, neither of us would stand for one another cheating. We took our wedding vows very seriously" she threw in.

"But happily married doesn't always equate to happily faithful. I understand that the large majority of people take their wedding vows seriously Claire, but then look at your friend Natalya. She and her husband both gave the impression they were happily married. Cat told me that she too was happily married. You are happily married but are you happy in yourself? Have you gotten everything you signed up for with your marriage? " it was a psychological question, one that Carly had been humming and harring whether to use or not, but she needed to get inside Claire's head, to understand her motive if they could prove it was definitely her who had gone off to the river with Billy and who had returned to her car alone.

DCI James Sidhu made an excuse to leave the interview room, and they noted it for the record. He wanted to contact PC Gold and ask him to arrange a search of the rubbish and the recycling bins in the area. Carly temporarily suspended the interview but didn't make any move to leave or hint that Claire could leave the room either. Instead she sat quietly whilst her boss went off. She watched Claire's reaction to the interview being stopped. Claire looked worried, but was doing her best to try and hide it. Carly had all the time in the world but only one chance to get a clear and definite admission from Claire. She couldn't afford to screw it up and she needed Claire to open up about everything. This was her perfect opportunity to plan the next steps of the interrogation during the break, to get the responses she now so desperately wanted. Her boss returned a few minutes later, and brought fresh tea with him for the three of them.

The minute that the tape was switched back on, Carly continued with her line of questioning "Did you want a relationship with Billy?" she asked in a sympathetic way, head slightly tilted and soft eyes that managed to burn right into Claire.

Claire blushed, took her new cup of tea and stared into it watching the liquid swirl gently around the china as she was much more careful not to spill it this time. She didn't answer but that was fine, Carly had all her questions and comments lined up.

"I think you were jealous of Natalya ", Carly continued. "I think you wanted to be in her shoes, to have what she had. You wanted to be that other woman to Billy, the one getting the attention." she stopped and looked at Claire with a glint of compassion. She understood how people reacted when they were infatuated with something. She had experienced people doing all sorts of crazy things, convincing themselves that it was in the name of love. She had witnessed fires, kidnappings, damage to property and cars. But she had never seen a murder in the name of passion. Not in the quiet little town of Oldcoewood, things like that didn't happen around here. Of course she had read numerous books, fiction and non-fiction on the subject, and she knew that it wasn't uncommon, but still it was a shock that it was happening in her own sleepy town. She was feeling confident though now that she was headed down the right track and just needed that final confirmation from Claire to bang the nail in the coffin.

"Your car matches that of the car we followed on CCTV. We have footage of a car picking Billy up and driving to the car park by the nursery near the river. My team are just pulling together the warrant to search your car now, I'll let you know when we have that. We also have footage of someone helping him to climb through the hedges into the field, in order to avoid the cameras on the main road. Avoiding the route that one would normally take to get to the river. That someone is you, isn't it Claire?"

"I want my solicitor," Claire whispered after a few minutes. Carly was gutted, of course, that was Claire's right but she was so, so close to getting a quick confession from her, and was even more curious as to the details behind it all.

As Claire hadn't formally been arrested, they had to let her go home. It was agreed that she would be back at 9.30 the following morning with her solicitor. This time they made sure that she understood that if she didn't turn up she would be arrested either way. DCI James Sidhu escorted Claire out of the interview room and to the front reception. He showed her the warrant to search her car, which she reluctantly nodded in acknowledgement of. He told her that her car was there at the station and would she like to call someone for a lift or could he arrange for one of his team to drive her home. Claire had turned a paler shade of white as she muttered that she would welcome the offer of a ride home. She thanked the Inspector and sat down to wait. She was struggling to keep her brave face on, but pleased that she had asked for her solicitor. She didn't actually know the person who was to come in to represent her in the morning, having never required the service before, and randomly picking a male name from a list provided for her, but a small part of her hoped that this person would be her saviour. In the meantime she had to go home and tell her husband what was going on. As she got in the car, she manufactured her story, naturally putting herself in the role of the victim.

Carly and James sat back down in their office to discuss the interview that had just taken place. "It seems too easy," Carly said as she dunked her fourth bourbon biscuit into her tea.

"But you've done a good job, researched well and that is why we brought her in." her boss exclaimed, just as Daniel walked in with some further information about Debbie Katz.

"Her route checks out!" he said. We have clear footage of her sitting on her own at one of the tables on the ferry. She ordered a cheese toasted sandwich and a can of coke, paid by card and we have the record. "I'm sorry, but she's not a suspect any more," he said as he slumped in his chair, worn down by the mental energy he had consumed.

"Not to worry," James replied. "Thank you for doing that, it was good work Daniel, but I think we might have our suspect. Unfortunately Mrs Edwards has requested a solicitor, so we are on hold until tomorrow, but let's see how we get on then. In the meantime you both look dreadful, so go home and have a rest."

"Well, thanks Boss" Carly pretended to look offended as she shoved the last of the biscuit in her mouth and stood up to pack her bag.

23.

Claire returned home, asking the officer to drop her off at the end of the road, allowing her to walk up to her house alone, and quickly got back into her routine of being the perfect mother and housewife. She prepared dinner and sat with her boys whilst they did their homework. Wayne came home and she told the boys they were free to do whatever they wanted.

"Where's your car?" was the first thing that Wayne asked her when he had changed out of his work clothes.

"I need to talk to you quite urgently" She ignored his question and poured him a large whiskey. He took the drink and they sat in the lounge. Claire positioned herself so that she wasn't directly facing Wayne but could turn her head for maximum effect.

"I've been to the police station today" she started. Wayne wasn't surprised, they were all having their turn at being interviewed. "But there's something I didn't tell you before," she hesitated.

"What is it?" Wayne turned to her abruptly.

"Well," she continued as she lowered her eyes. "I didn't tell you that Billy had attacked me. He sexually assaulted me" she dropped her head down towards her lap.

"What the hell?" Wayne looked at her "When did this happen? Why didn't you tell me? The bastard, I would have killed him myself if I knew that."

"That's why I didn't tell you" Claire forced a tear to drop, pleased that she had chopped up the onions rather than using pre-chopped ones from the freezer for dinner. "I just wanted to forget all about it"

"But when did that happen? How did that happen?" Wayne took his wife's hand in his own.

"It happened at Christmas time," Claire found it easy to tell her story "at Patrick and Fi's house. I can't actually remember how it started but I think I went to the bathroom to do my hair and then the next thing I knew was him standing behind me. He had locked the door and he had this big grin on his face. I laughed and asked him what he was doing, and do you know what he replied, Wayne? He said to me I'm doing you next. So vulgar I know. I told him to piss off but he came towards me and pinned me against the sink as he lifted my dress up and pushed his hands inside my knickers. Inside me. He attacked me, Wayne".

Wayne was silent, thinking over what his wife had just told him. Still holding her hand, he eventually commented "Weren't you wearing a trouser suit at Patrick's? I remember you showing it to me as you tried to hide the label under the bed."

Claire looked up at Wayne, shocked at his memory of her wardrobe choices. "No, no" she stumbled, "that was a different night. I was wearing my, um, my black dress with the lace sleeves, you know the one? But anyway, what I was wearing doesn't matter my darling. He attacked me, he assaulted me. I was petrified!"

"But you didn't scream out, or kick out when it happened? And you didn't make us leave straight afterwards?" Wayne looked genuinely confused.

"Well now, it all happened so quickly. He put his hand over my mouth to stop me from talking whilst the other hand was roaming. Afterwards I went straight to the kitchen for a drink, I wanted to forget the awful ordeal"

"Did you climax?" Wayne's questions were getting out of hand. He was not reacting how she wanted him to.

"Of course not!" Claire spat angrily at him, wishing that her story had been true and that of course she had climaxed. "I was scared Wayne, I was trying to push him away"

"Yet you had two spare hands and two spare feet as he had one hand over your mouth and the other inside you. And a big woman like you couldn't push a pissed Billy off?" he removed his hand from hers, cupping his whiskey glass in both hands.

"I swear Wayne, I swear it's the truth. He attacked me and now I've had to go and tell the police about it all."

"Why have you told the police that? What relevance does it have in Billy's death?" he queried.

"Because apparently, just before Billy died, he told Cat." She lied some more, "and Cat asked me if it was true and now I have to tell the police because they want to know if Cat killed him."

"Cat didn't kill him" Wayne muttered as he now got up and walked over to the other side of the room. "She was too weak, too worn down. She might have got someone to do it for her, but I don't think she could have done it herself. Cat is a good woman. She wouldn't hurt a fly."

Why was Wayne protecting Cat? Claire was beyond unhinged now, and thoughts were flying through her head. She almost forgot about the story she was fabricating herself to try and frame her friend, it was back firing. Was Wayne having an affair with Cat? Did he have something to do with Billy's death? Obviously these thoughts were crazy but where was the sympathy she wanted from her husband too. She was expecting him to go crazy but not at her, at Billy! It was all going wrong, and now she had to prepare what she was going to tell her solicitor first thing the next morning to keep her visit to the police as short as possible.

"And where is the car anyway?" Wayne repeated.

"It's at the police station," Claire replied sheepishly. "I was so shaken up after my visit there to tell them this, that I felt I couldn't drive home. So one of the kind officers gave me a lift. I'll collect it in the morning. It wouldn't hurt the children to walk to school for once. It's not far!"

The next morning, after telling the children they had to get themselves to school she decided to walk the mile and a half to the police station in the centre of town. She was so pleased that she had thoroughly cleaned her car, and was sure there was nothing they could uncover. Her solicitor was an old man, he looked like he didn't want to be there and was purely going through the motions and avoiding all of her emotions. Claire hated him. She needed him to feel for her, and help her come up with an answer that would allow her to leave as soon as possible. He was more interested in finding the facts in order to put his case together and be able to represent her in court, if it came to that.

PC Carly Cook and DCI James Sidhu turned up exactly on time, looking refreshed and ready for their day ahead. Much the opposite of Claire who was already sweating from her walk and shaking from too much caffeine.

DCI Sidhu started off the meeting by introducing all the parties and confirming the date and time for the recording. He summarised their conversation from the day before and waited for Claire's solicitor, Brian Fairchild to comment and make notes.

"And so" Carly took over the next stage of the questioning. "We have a strong belief that it was your car seen driving Billy to the car park by the nursery and near the river. We have an image of a person, who quite easily matches your profile taking Billy though the hedgerow towards the river, via the fields." She showed Claire and her solicitor the CCTV footage and watched closely for Claire's reaction before she sprang her next well-rehearsed line on her.

"I think you led him to the river to have sex with him," she paused for a moment to see Claire's recognition creep across her face, "and when he didn't respond or reciprocate to your suggestions, you got angry with him and strangled him". She paused. "At what point did you hit him with the rock though, was that before or after you strangled him?" she calmly sat back in her chair and waited.

Brian Fairchild turned to his client. "You've not been placed under arrest, you do not need to say anything that you don't want to."

But Claire was exhausted, the fight was gone. Her husband didn't believe her, she didn't think he even liked her any more. She had nothing left to lose, and now she was ready to talk.

"Even in the horrifically pissed state he was in, and I know I looked really good when I picked him up, he still wouldn't fuck me" Claire whispered. "Why? What is wrong with me that he couldn't even take me up on a free offer" she started to sob "I literally handed it to him on a plate. A huge, sodding plate with me in the centre of it. I planned the whole night. We were going to have so much fun, he was going to make me feel fucking amazing. We were going to have one night of pure lust and then I would ignore him. Just like he did with Nat. Fucking bastard deserved it. He made a fool out of me, the bastard. Happy enough for me to give him a blow job while my husband and our friends were in the next room, happy for me to pull him off in his own bedroom and then he walked away and left me to clear up the mess. Clear up his bedroom, his mess on my body . He went back to his wife, happy as fucking Larry. He got exactly what he wanted and then left me in a situation where if I were found, I would have looked just awful. He was ok though. He went back to his wife, gave her a slap on the arse or something and then probably went off to fuck Nat after using me. He happily shagged her, made her feel wanted and made her feel special. Put a smile on her stupid smug botoxed face. But no, with me he just used me and walked away. That's not playing fair" She finally looked up at Carly and her boss, raised her eyebrows and added "That's what you wanted to hear, isn't it?"

"Playing Fair?" Carly ticked the final box on her checksheet. "But why did you keep going back for more?" Carly persisted. "I don't understand why you would push for someone so out of reach, when you have so much better at home. Why did you keep going after someone who had rejected you so vulgarly? You have Wayne, you love Wayne, and I'm sure Wayne loves you. So why did you continually go after Billy?". That's what she couldn't understand. It was so demoralising, so degrading. Why would anyone allow themselves to be humiliated so greatly and still try and go back for more?

"I had to win. I had to get him just once, and then I would have ruined him. I would have ruined his life, his work, his marriage." Claire was bitter as she quietly spat out her answer. "It was like an addiction. Like a lottery ticket where you are just one number away from a win, you have to go back and try again. He made me think it would happen, he would look at me and smile. He'd wink at me and brush past me, he led me on but he just used me. Once I realised that he was using me, I had to win. I'm better than them, I deserved to get what I wanted but I didn't."

"And so you killed him?" Carly looked over to her recorder to make sure it was definitely recording the conversation.

"Cat isn't upset, you know. She hated him too" Claire responded, not answering the question. "I did her a favour! She wasn't going to leave him because she didn't want to leave our group. We're all she has down here and she needs us. I had to make him leave her."

"Claire Edwards, I am arresting you for the murder of William Ashton. You do not have to say anything, but it may harm your defence if you do not mention when questioned, something that you later rely on in Court. Anything you do say may be given in evidence. Do you understand?"

Claire nodded, almost relieved that her story was now out, and Carly confirmed her affirmation for the recording. "Do you want to tell me the whole story? Right from the beginning?" Carly continued.

Claire did. She looked over at her solicitor and shrugged. Maybe he could get her a lesser sentence because she was being nice now. But she was so tired, she was well and truly caught. Despite having thought that she might have got away with murder, she had been so riled by her visit to Natalya, she realised that she had put herself into a corner from which she could never back out. It was time to put an end to the secrets and lies. Maybe if he was a good solicitor he could reduce her sentence on mental health grounds. She made sure that she shed a few tears as she told her story to the police and her solicitor.

Claire knew that Billy was going out on that Friday night, her own husband had been invited along too, but she had persuaded Wayne to stay in with her instead and have a takeaway. She needed him as far away from the setting as she could. This had to have nothing to do with him at all, because she did love him very much, and was hoping to return home after the event to carry on her life as normal. Of course she now realised that wasn't to be.

Claire had managed to get some sleeping pills from someone she knew at the coffee shop in the gym and had ground them up to put in Wayne's wine. She kept topping up his glass, whilst nursing her own first glass and pretending to act as drunk as her husband was. It didn't take long for Wayne to pass out on the sofa, and for her to check that the children were still oblivious to the world around them whilst gaming in their rooms.

She had dressed in a kinky leather outfit she had bought from a shop in East London. She didn't want to risk buying anything online or anything local so had made the trip a few weeks before, when the boys were at school and Wayne was at work. She had hidden her purchase in the boot of her car, inside the spare tyre. She had been proud of how well she was covering her tracks this far. She put her thick raincoat on, aware of the material it was made of, so that no fibres from her favourite wool coat could be transferred and she covered her car number-plates with carrier bags. She had planned everything meticulously, checking and double checking that it could not be traced back to her, and this was just to have one night of sex. Once. But with her friend's husband and her husband's friend. She wasn't planning an horrific murder.

With Wayne passed out and the boys on their computers, she quietly left the house, making sure that the outside lights were switched off and rolled the car down the driveway before turning the engine on as quietly as she could and driving into town. She drove around the block a couple of times before spotting Billy. It had been easy to see him wandering down the road after he left the pub, and she was pleased that he was on his own. That had been a big worry, had he still been with Lee and Richard, she would have had to act a lot closer to his home as he lived just a road away from Richard's house. But as it was, she was in luck, and when she pulled the car over and called his name, he was grateful for the lift. She thought that if she was spotted on camera, she was innocently offering a lift to a friend in need. Being out in the centre of town gave her more options of where to take Billy and as the roads were quiet, but she chose the river where it would be dark, and should anyone walk past they might just turn their noses up at the public display of affection but not much more. She wasn't the first, and she certainly wouldn't be the last to have drunken sex by the river. As she drove Billy to the carpark she loosened her coat so that he could see what she was wearing underneath. He didn't react at all which made her angry. She needed his reaction, she needed his attention. She moved her hand onto his lap, and gently rubbed his leg, working closer and closer towards his groin. He relaxed back into the seat of the car, his legs opening wider as he let her stroke him, a satisfied grin on his drunken face. This wasn't her plan. Tonight was about her and not him so she took her hand away again and concentrated on driving.

Billy had been a bit weary of climbing through the hedge, he started to argue about getting his shirt dirty but Claire had persuaded him it was the best idea and he was really too drunk not to follow her. She whispered to him as they were climbing through what she would like to do to him when they were alone, and he seemed happier to follow. When they reached the river, after walking around the perimeter of the field, she removed her coat completely, but left her leather gloves on and moved within inches of Billy. He finally could see what was on offer, and had enjoyed looking at her. Greedily he took her hand to massage his groin as he got harder. But still he didn't touch her body in return. Claire had stripped off Billy's clothes, until he was standing by the river bank in his boxer shorts, and she moved in to crouch down in front of Billy to give him a blow job. It didn't take long for Billy to get over excited and Claire had finished him off in minutes. She took his hands and placed them on her breasts but still he didn't respond. He wobbled backwards drunkenly and his hands fell away. It was all too much for Claire, and finally she had shouted at him, she had asked him what the hell was wrong and why he didn't want to fuck her, why he didn't want to pleasure her as she had done to him.

Billy had drunkenly slurred in her face "I don't think you're very sexy. You're a bit fat for me you silly bitch, but you give great head. So you can be my blow jobber." He had laughed at his own rendition of his wording but Claire didn't smile back. She was humiliated, insulted and ashamed. She pulled her mac back on and Billy turned to find his own clothes. He bent down to try and get his jeans on and that was when she picked up a rock and smashed it over the back of Billy's head. She was crying with shame but still she found it so much easier than she thought. Billy wavered and tried to hold himself steady but failed and fell. He looked up at Claire, confused now and very dizzy. Claire gently knelt down next to him, looked him straight in the eye and with her gloved hands, stretched her fingers around his throat. Again, it didn't seem as difficult as she had anticipated as she squeezed her hands tighter and tighter together. Billy made a slight effort to stop her but she slapped him around the face and his head fell back onto the ground. She was strong for someone who did very little muscle work in the gym and of course she was sober, compared to him being hammered. She returned both hands to grip his neck as hard as she could and watched as his eyes bulged and he tried to call out. Something had taken over her, an out of body experience and she felt as if she was watching from afar. She couldn't stop herself from finishing the job. For the final moment of Billy's life, Claire shut her eyes and squeezed as hard as she could. She knew when he was dead, as the muscles in his neck relaxed. She opened her eyes in horror and looked at what she had done. Without thinking she pushed his body into the river and quickly tidied up the area, sweeping up the clothing in her arms. She looked around but heard no other sounds, still she kept close to the hedges as she made her way back to her car, and as soon as she was in her car she took a bin liner from the boot to put her outfit and his clothes in and sat in the car, in the dark of the car park whilst she changed out of her leathers and put on a tracksuit that she'd left in a bag on the backseat. She was crying now, but she wasn't sure if it was out of fear or humiliation. Strangely, she didn't feel guilty. She felt that she had done the right thing. Billy wasn't going to ruin her life any more, he wasn't going to abuse her or make a fool out of her, and she certainly wasn't going to make a fool out of herself again just for his attention. It was time to go home, but she didn't want to drive the obvious route home, she had to make a detour. Claire drove to Coes Green and made an effort to drive down the single track lanes that were least likely to have cameras on them. She wanted to get to Molville to dump her bag. Molville was a big town and a bin bag of clothes would be less likely to be discovered. The following day she cleaned her car out and filled another bag with all the rubbish that might have fingerprints on, that was the bag she dumped on her way to see Richard at his office.

Despite being recorded, Carly still made some notes in her book. This woman was just a regular mum and wife living in the sleepy town of Oldcoewood, but she was a killer, and had constructed her actions, whilst her family were unaware at home. She had murdered someone purely for rejecting her advances and making her look stupid, and then returned home to look after his widow and be a shoulder to cry on. Not only that, but she then moved on to try and blackmail Billy's lover in an attempt to boost her own self-confidence and status in a clique of parents who probably didn't care who was doing what, as long as the drink was flowing.

As Carly put the handcuffs on Claire and her colleague led her away to the cells to be processed before moving to prison, she couldn't help but ask Claire a couple more questions "Do you regret it Claire?"

"I regret trying to win him," Claire answered "But I don't regret defending myself. No one treats me the way he did. I regret that I won't see my boys grow up and I'm sad for Wayne because he's really done nothing wrong. I need Psychiatric help, I know that's what's wrong with me. You see that don't you Carly? I just wanted everyone to Play Fair" She was already planning her next move, the one in which she claims mental health issues, which could reduce her sentence.

"Just one more question" Carly was concluding their interview, she was exhausted and wanted to head home for a hot bath and an afternoon curled up on the sofa with her favourite fluffy pal. "Facebook. Are you Finn Dunn? Was that a clue for us?"

"Yes that was me"

"But why did you post on Facebook?"

"Pure boredom to be honest with you. I knew they wouldn't know it was me, I wanted to keep everyone on their toes. I'm a hell of a lot smarter than the others. I was playing with them. I wanted to scare Cat, make her open her eyes and look around her, instead of climbing under her rock and hoping everything would just go away"

"But you weren't playing fair yourself, were you Claire? Murder isn't fair play!"

Claire shrugged, she had nothing more to say. She had all the time in the world now to think and wonder if it was all worth it. She was still a victim, that she knew at least.

Carly handed Claire over to her colleague and turned back towards her office. She was just happy that she had caught her killer and could hopefully bring some normality back to the small urban town where nothing ever happens.

24.

THREE MONTHS LATER

Cat was pleased that it hadn't taken long to sell her home. She had sold it to a lovely young couple with a baby on the way. They would love the area, love the schools and the playgrounds and hopefully also find some solid friends to build relationships with. She was sad that she was having to move her boys out of two great schools, and that Ned wouldn't be starting at one of the best secondary schools in the area that she had fought so hard to get a place for him at, but with the money she had received from Billy's life assurance she would be able to pay for private schools up in Northampton, near to her parents, where the house prices were much more affordable and she could now live mortgage free.

Cat was looking forward to a fresh new start. Her parents were more than happy that she was moving back closer to them, and she knew that the boys would settle down with time. They were young enough to build new friendships, and away from their previous lives they wouldn't be asked or judged whenever they went out. But she also knew that in order to do this, she had to cut ties with everyone in Oldcoewood. The friendship group was toxic, and after Claire had been arrested, she couldn't bear to face the others. They had tried to be supportive, but Cat could tell that it was lip service. They were still friendly with Natalya, despite having heard the full story of Billy's affair. These were women who just needed to belong somewhere, and they would sacrifice their morals and their beliefs for that. Natalya was still with Richard, although only just. She was having to do everything in her power to rebuild her own marriage. Richard was now the injured party. The one left standing after everyone else had departed. He was the one who had to still wake up each morning and look over at his wife who had cheated on him with one of his best friends. He wasn't going to forgive Natalya but at the same time he still loved her, and was prepared to give things time to change. The relationship naturally was strained though, and Natalya, whilst still trying to do everything she could to make Richard happier, knew that it would take months, even years for her to redeem herself in any way. She was going to have to be on her best behaviour from now on, focus on bringing up the children, supporting her husband and keeping away from anyone else's.

Wayne had filed for divorce from Claire as soon as he discovered what had happened. He was naturally distraught and extremely shocked. He hadn't seen any of this coming, hadn't suspected a thing, because Claire had been such a good actress all the way. In fact, in hindsight, Wayne realised that the last few years had all been a charade with her, a production in which she was the leading lady, the damsel in distress, the boss of the mafia and supportive first lady. Wayne was grateful for the support from his friends. He would need them around him more; the men to give him the moral support he wanted more than anything; the rugby club to keep him and his boys busy; the women to help him with the children, as he didn't have a clue as to what Claire had previously done. The when's, the where's, the how's and the with who's. Thankfully, the other women were involved enough in his life to know all the answers and had no problem tagging his children along with their own. Something he would be eternally grateful for and would have to work out a way to show his appreciation, as soon as he had a minute to think for himself. Jen and Fiona set up a rota for them to take the boys back to their own houses after school and clubs, and would make sure they had a good evening meal, whilst Wayne tried to get back into work. He still had to work hard and concentrate on selling his conservatories. The sympathy from his boss had worn off after the newspapers got bored with printing details about his wife and he still had a mortgage to pay off. He did think about moving away from the area, but the fact was, that he himself had not put a foot wrong, he didn't want to look guilty for something his wife had done, and he didn't want to have to lose his whole life for her actions.

The rest of the group were quiet for a while. Other than the offers of help for Wayne, and a few quiet drinks for the men to go out, it wasn't a time to be having parties and social gatherings. The women didn't want to be seen instigating events with Natalya, although she was trying tremendously hard to get at least one in the diary, to bring any element of normality back to her own shamed life. Cat had made it quite clear that she didn't want to hear from any of them, despite the numerous efforts at the beginning from the other women. But the endeavours to get Cat out, even for a coffee, were short lived as the other women realised they were getting nowhere. Instead they would text occasionally, send their thoughts and wishes, and move on with their own lives. At any rate, the kids had come to the end of another school year, some of them were going off to the same secondary school together but there were no big parties outside of the organised school one to celebrate this. And when Natalya messaged to say that her daughter was going to a different school to the other kids, no one responded.

Claire was taken to prison, kicking and screaming to be psychoanalysed for her mental state, but whilst she was waiting to hear about her own future, she wasted no time in writing a letter to Cat. She still couldn't accept that it was her fault, and so she pinned all the blame on Natalya and Billy. She explained how she was pushed to try and compete with Nat for Billy's attention, completely ignorant of the fact she was writing to Billy's widow. She wrote in great detail of all the things she had found out about the affair, she didn't care what Cat would think any more, she just wanted to try and maintain her belief that she was still innocent in some way. She wrote three pages of self-obsessed drivel, but it didn't matter anyway, as when the letter arrived and Cat could see the postmark, the letter and envelope went straight into the shredder and the shredder emptied into the outside bin.

Carly took a week off work following the case. She hadn't realised how worn out she was from it. Despite it all being wrapped up in record time, the mental energy and lack of sleep had caught up with her. She switched her phone off for the first day anyway but then decided she was missing the action too much. She called in to Daniel to see what was going on. "Carly, you're on leave" he replied. "Get off your phone and go and do something exciting."

"I just want to know what I'm missing whilst I'm away" she answered with a small snigger. "Fine", he responded. "If you want to come back to work early, we have a case you can manage. Fly tipping down Catkins Lane" he laughed. Carly hung up, she had a wall to redecorate anyway after removing all the blu tack and seeing the marks left on it. She would leave the fly tipping in the safe hands of one of her colleagues.

THANK YOU

I really hope you have enjoyed my first novel, Play Fair. It was written as a challenge to myself but soon became my go to for times when I wanted to release both my own emotions and all my energy and I love to watch the words appear on my screen in front of me. Plans for the next novel are well and truly underway and I hope to share that with you soon.

To get this book going, I forgot to make dinner for the family on many occasions, and I would like to thank my darling Husband and my beautiful daughters for the repeated chicken nuggets and chips that he had to cook for them.

I am also eternally grateful for my mother, my brother and sister in law who have encouraged me at every step of the way and provided me with that can-do attitude.

My dog has patiently sat by my side through my writing experience and the breaks to take him walkies have kept me sane.

Finally I want to thank my dearest friends who have also been a great source of encouragement and gin, to get this to the end.

If you have enjoyed reading Play Fair, please give me a review, and if you haven't, well, we could talk about it, but remember you would be offending my 4th child!

Alexis

Printed in Great Britain
by Amazon

66058515R00111